Anonymous

Romances of the Reign of Henry II

The Valois romances; the d'Artagnan romances; the Regency romances; the Marie

Antoinette romances; the Count of Monte Cristo, etc.

Anonymous

Romances of the Reign of Henry II
The Valois romances; the d'Artagnan romances; the Regency romances; the Marie Antoinette romances; the Count of Monte Cristo, etc.

ISBN/EAN: 9783337050214

Printed in Europe, USA, Canada, Australia, Japan

Cover: Foto ©Andreas Hilbeck / pixelio.de

More available books at **www.hansebooks.com**

ROMANCES OF THE REIGN OF HENRI II.; THE VALOIS
'' ROMANCES; THE D'ARTAGNAN ROMANCES; THE
REGENCY ROMANCES; THE MARIE ANTOINETTE
ROMANCES; THE COUNT OF MONTE CRISTO, ETC.

BY

ALEXANDRE DUMAS.

INTRODUCTORY NOTES

AND

LISTS OF CHARACTERS.

BOSTON:
LITTLE, BROWN, AND COMPANY.
1895.

UNIVERSITY PRESS :
JOHN WILSON AND SON, CAMBRIDGE, U. S. A.

CONTENTS.

4   CONTENTS.

THE TWO DIANAS.

INTRODUCTORY NOTE.

THE claim of Alexandre Dumas to be considered first among historical romancists, past or present, can hardly be disputed; and his magic pen finds abundant, rich material for the historical setting of the tale told in the following pages. The period in which the action of "The Two Dianas" is supposed to take place, covers the later years of Henri II. and the brief and melancholy reign of his oldest son, François II., the ill-fated husband of Mary Stuart, whose later history has caused her brief occupancy of the throne of France to be lost sight of. This period saw the germination and early maturity, if not the actual sowing, of the spirit of the Reformation in France. It was during these years that the name of John Calvin acquired the celebrity which has never waned, and that his devoted followers, La Renaudie, Théodore de Bèze, Ambroise Paré, the famous surgeon, and the immortal Coligny began the crusade for freedom of worship which was steadily maintained, unchecked by Tumult of Amboise, or Massacre of St. Bartholomew, until

Henri of Navarre put the crown upon their heroic labors, and gave them respite for a time with the famous "Edict of Nantes," made more famous still by its "Revocation" a century later under the auspices of Madame de Maintenon, at the instigation of her Jesuit allies. Those portions of the story which introduce us to the councils of the Reformers are none the less interesting because the characters introduced are actual historical personages, nor can it fail to add interest to the encounter between La Renaudie and Pardaillan to know that it really took place, and that the two men had previously been to each other almost nearer than brothers. It was but one of innumerable heart-rending incidents, inseparable from all civil and religious conflicts, but in which those presided over by the Florentine mother of three Valois kings of France were prolific beyond belief.

How closely the author has adhered to historical fact for the groundwork of his tale, will appear by comparing it with one of Balzac's *Études Philosophiques*, entitled "Sur Catherine de Médicis," the first part of which covers the same period as "The Two Dianas," and describes many of the same events; the variations are of the slightest.

The patient forbearance of Catherine de Médicis, under the neglect of her husband, and the arrogant presumption of Diane de Poitiers, abetted by the

Constable de Montmorency; her swift and speedy vengeance upon them as soon as she was left a widow with her large brood of possible kings; her jealous fear of the influence of the Duc de Guise and his brother the Cardinal de Lorraine, which led her to desire the death of her eldest son, the unfortunate François, because his queen was the niece of the powerful and ambitious brothers, and which also led her to oppose their influence by a combination with two such incongruous elements as the Constable Montmorency and the Protestant Bourbon princes of Navarre, remaining all the while the bitterest foe that the reformed religion ever had, — all these, as described in the following pages, are strictly in conformity with historical fact. So, too, is the story of the defence of St. Quentin in its main details, and of the siege of Calais, where the Duc de Guise did receive the terrible wound which caused the sobriquet of *Le Balafré* to be applied to him, and was cured by the skilful hand of Master Ambroise Paré. So of the Tumult of Amboise, and the painful scenes attending the execution of the victims; and so, finally, of the scene at the death-bed of François II., the controversy between the shrinking conservatism of the King's regular medical advisers, and the daring eclecticism of Paré, proposing to perform the "new operation" of trepanning. It may, perhaps, be said

that the Chancellor de l'Hôpital is made to appear
in too unfavorable a light; he certainly was something far above the mere bond-slave of Catherine de
Médicis.

Dumas himself tells us what basis of truth there
is for the sometimes amusing, sometimes serious,
but always intensely interesting confusion between
Martin-Guerre and his unscrupulous double.

Nowhere, it may be said, in history or romance,
is there to be found so touching a glimpse as this
of poor Mary Stuart.   Here we see naught save the
lovely and lovable side of the unfortunate queen,
without a hint of the fatal weakness which, as it
developed in the stormy later years of her life,
made her marvellous beauty and charm the instru-
ments of her ruin.

So much for those portions of " The Two Dianas "
which rest upon a basis of fact. History records
further that Henri II. was accidentally killed in
friendly jousting by the Comte de Montgommery;
but with that history ends and romance begins.
The personage whom Monsieur Dumas presents to
us under that title perhaps never existed; but let
the reader be the judge, after reading of the pure
and sacred but unhappy love of Gabriel de Montgommery and Diane de Castro, if a lovelier gem of
fiction was ever enclosed in an historical setting.

THE TWO DIANAS.

LIST OF CHARACTERS.

Period, 1521–1574.

FRANÇOIS I., King of France.
HENRI II., his successor.
CATHERINE DE MÉDICIS, Queen to Henri II.
THE DAUPHIN, afterwards François II.
HENRI, his brother, afterwards Henri III.
MARY STUART, married to the Dauphin.
MARY, Queen of England.
DUC D'ORLÉANS, afterwards Charles IX.
MARGUERITE DE FRANCE, sister of Henri II.
MARGUERITE DE VALOIS, daughter of Henri II.
PRINCESS ÉLISABETH.
FRANÇOIS, Duc d'Alençon.
DUC DE GUISE, Lieutenant-General of France.
MONSEIGNEUR LE CARDINAL DE LORRAINE, his brother.
DUC D'AUMALE, brother of Duc de Guise.
MARQUIS D'ELBŒUF,
MARQUIS DE VAUDEMONT,   officers of Duc de Guise.
MONSIEUR DE BIRON,
MONSIEUR DE THERMES,
CONSTABLE ANNE DE MONTMORENCY.
FRANÇOIS DE MONTMORENCY, his son.
ANTOINE DE NAVARRE.
LOUIS DE BOURBON, Prince de Condé, his brother.

PHILIP II., of Spain.

PHILIBERT EMMANUEL, Duc de Savoie.

ADMIRAL GASPARD DE COLIGNY.

CAPTAIN OGER,
MONSIEUR DE LAUXFORD, an engineer,
MONSIEUR DE RAMBOUILLET,
MONSIEUR DE BREUIL,
BARON DE VAULPERGUES,
} French officers serving with the Admiral.

MADAME DE BRÈZE, Duchesse de Valentinois, commonly called Diane de Poitiers, mistress of Henri II.

DIANE, Duchesse de Castro, afterwards Duchesse d'Angoulême, daughter of Henri II. and Diane de Poitiers.

MADAME DE LEVISTON, in attendance on Diane de Castro.

HORACE FARNÈSE, Duc de Castro.

MADAME D'ÉTAMPES, mistress of François I.

GABRIEL, Seigneur de Lorge, Vicomte de Montgommery, styling himself Vicomte d'Exmés, in love with Diane de Castro.

JACQUES, Comte de Montgommery, Gabriel's father, imprisoned by Henri II.

MASTER ELYOT, intendant of the County of Montgommery.

PERROT TRAVIGNY, squire to the Comte de Montgommery.

MARTIN-GUERRE, Gabriel's squire.

BERTRANDE ROLLES, wife of Martin-Guerre.

ALOYSE, Gabriel's nurse.

ENGUERRAND LORIEN, squire of the Counts of Vimoutiers.

ARNAULD DU THILL, Martin-Guerre's double, in the secret service of Constable de Montmorency.

MONSIEUR DE BOISSY, Grand Equerry of France.

MONSIEUR DE SALVOISON, governor of the Châtelet Prison.

MONSIEUR DE SAZERAC, his successor.

MONSIEUR DE LANGEAIS,
MONSIEUR DE BOUTIÈRES,
COMTE DE SANCERRE,
MONSIEUR D'AUSSUN,
MONSIEUR D'ENGHIEN,
COMTE DE MONTAUSIER,
} gentlemen of the Court of François I.

MONSIEUR DE VIEILLEVILLE,
MONSIEUR LE COLONEL-GÉNÉRAL DE BONNIVET,
GASPARD DE TAVANNES,
COMTE DE POMMERIVE,
MARÉCHAL D'ANVILLE,
MONSIEUR DE BURI,
} gentlemen of the Court of Henri II.

PRÉSIDENT BERTRAND,
CHANCELLOR OLIVIER DE LENVILLE,
COMTE D'AUMALE,
MONSIEUR DE SEDAN,
MONSIEUR DE HUMIÈRES,
MONSIEUR DE SAINT-ANDRÉ,
COMTE DE SAINT-REMY,
} of the King's council.

RICHELIEU, captain of arquebusiers.

MONSIEUR D'AVALLON, captain of the guards of Henri II.

JACQUES AMYOT, the preceptor of the princes.

LADY LENNOX,
MADAME DE CONI,
} governesses of the princesses.

MADAME DAYELLE, lady-in-waiting to Mary Stuart.

NICOLAS DUVAL, a councillor of Parliament.

JACQUES DE SAVOIE, Duc de Nemours,
ALPHONSE D'ESTE, Duc de Ferrara,
} knights in the tournament at which Henri II. was killed.

AMBROISE PARÉ, surgeon.

CHANCELLOR DE L'HÔPITAL.

BRANTÔME, historian.

ANTOINE DE BAÏF, dramatic writer.

RÉMY BELLEAU, a poet.

MARÉCHAL PIERRE STROZZI, an engineer of the sixteenth century.

FLORIMOND, an usher at the French court.

JACINTHE,
DÉNISE,
} waiting-maids to Diane de Castro.

NOSTRADAMUS, astrologer and physician.

JOHN CALVIN.

THÉODORE DE BÈZE, historian of the Reformed Church.

BARON DE LA RENAUDIE, a Huguenot officer.

BARON DE PARDAILLAN, an officer of the king's troops.

DAVID, a Calvinistic minister.

DES AVENELLES, advocate, a traitor to the Calvinists.

BARON CASTELNAU DE CHALOSSES,
COMTE DE VILLEMANGIS,
COMTE DE MAZÈRES,
BARON DE RAUNAY,
} condemned Calvinists.

MONSIEUR DE BRAGUELONNE, Lieutenant of Police.

MASTER ARPION, his secretary.

LIGNIÈRES, an agent of police.

ANTOINE DE MOUCHY, otherwise styled Démocharès, Doctor of the Sorbonne and Canon of Noyon, Grand Inquisitor of the Faith in France.

JEAN PEUQUOY, syndic of the weavers of St. Quentin.

PIERRE PEUQUOY, an armorer.

BABETTE, Pierre Peuquoy's sister.

LORD WENTWORTH, Governor of Calais.

LORD GREY, his brother-in-law, commanding the English archers.

LORD DERBY, an English officer.

SIR EDWARD FLEMING, herald of England.

ANSELME, a fisherman.

ANDRÉ, a page.

SISTER MONIQUE, Superior of the Benedictine convent at St. Quentin.

HEINRICH SCHARFENSTEIN,
PILLETROUSE,
FRANTZ SCHARFENSTEIN,
MALEMORT,
LACTANCE,
YVONNET,
AMBROSIO,
} officers and soldiers in Gabriel's service.

LANDRY,
CHESNEL,
AUBRIOT,
CONTAMINE,
BALU,
} veterans of the war in Lorraine, entering the service of Vicomte d'Exmés.

PAGE OF THE DUKE OF SAVOY.

INTRODUCTORY NOTE.

In "The Page of the Duke of Savoy" we meet again
most of the members of the doughty band of adven-
turers with whom Gabriel de Montgomery is said
in the "Two Dianas" to have accomplished the
marvellous feat of carrying the Old Fort of Calais
by escalade: Malemort, the seamed and scarred
hero of a hundred fights, whose first rush was
always so impetuous and reckless that he inevit-
ably received a fresh wound at the very beginning,
and was incapacitated for further service; Yvonnet
the dandy, bold as a lion by daylight, and timid as
a hare when the sun had gone down; Pilletrousse,
the rifler of dead men's pockets; Lactance, whose
excessive blood-thirstiness was only equalled by
his devoutness; and the two Scharfensteins, uncle
and nephew, whose feats of strength out-Hercules
Hercules. Procope, Maldent, and Fracasso are new
acquaintances, equally diverting, each in his particular line.

The period of this tale was crowded with events of deepest import to the world's history: it embraced the culmination of the world-empire of Charles V. and his abdication; the early years of the reign of Philip II., in which his future policy and conduct were so clearly foreshadowed; the struggle for supremacy between the Guises and Catherine de Médicis, the Florentine mother of the last three Valois Kings of France; and the irresistible growth and spread of the Reformation.

Of all the famous men who fought and governed in that age, perhaps the very noblest was Emmanuel Philibert, Duke of Savoy, whom Dumas selected as the central figure of his story. All that is here told us of him and his character is amply supported by authority.

Many of the historical events woven into the plot of the "Two Dianas" are here presented to us again, mainly in forms which follow the chronicles more closely. This is especially true of the life of the Comte de Montgomery, and the circumstances attending the fatal disaster at the Tournelles. There is no reason to believe that the death of Henri II. was the result of anything but pure accident, nor has history any more to say of the Comte de Montgomery than is said by our author in the following pages. It will be noticed, however, that the gloomy prognostications of Nostradamus reappear here in slightly different form.

As to the siege of Saint Quentin, too, the description given in the present work is entitled to the credit of being more nearly in accord with the facts than that which omits to mention Dandelot's presence, and makes Gaspard de Coligny play a subordinate part to Gabriel de Montgomery. It was the failure of Philip II. to follow up the fall of the town (inexplicable unless it was due to his jealousy of the Duke of Savoy) which saved Paris, and not the defence made by the garrison and citizens, heroic and devoted as their conduct was.

It would be perhaps more accurate to entitle "The Page of the Duke of Savoy" a part of the romance of history than an historical romance; for aside from the scenes in which the exploits of Procope and his associates appear, and the deeply touching love episode of Emmanuel Philibert and his pseudo-page, there are few chapters of which the historical accuracy can be impugned,— from the famous scene at Brussels when Charles V. laid down his sceptre, to his mock obsequies at the little convent in Spain; from Henri II. haughtily receiving the heralds of Spain and England, to

Henri II. meekly consenting to the shameful treaty of Cateau-Cambresis; from the brilliant pageant and superb jousting in the lists at the Tournelles, to the chamber of death, with Catherine de Médicis hovering jealously about the bed of the dying king, who had been so long and consistently unfaithful to her.

The epoch is one which readily lends itself to the romantic treatment, and under the hand of the master few opportunities of arousing the interest and moving the heart of the reader have been lost.

PAGE OF THE DUKE OF SAVOY.

LIST OF CHARACTERS.

Period, 1528–1580.

THE EMPEROR, Charles V.

MARY OF AUSTRIA, the Queen Dowager of Hungary, sister of Charles V.

MARY, Queen of England.

PHILIP, Prince of Spain, her husband, son of Charles V.

QUEEN ELEANOR, sister of Charles V.

DON CARLOS, the Emperor's grandson.

EMMANUEL PHILIBERT, Duc de Savoie, surnamed *Tête de Fer*, nephew of Charles V.

SCIANCA-FERRO, his squire.

GAETANO, his major-domo.

CHARLES THE GOOD, of Portugal, father of Emmanuel Philibert.

BEATRICE OF PORTUGAL, Emmanuel Philibert's mother.

LEONA MARAVIGLIA, passing as Leone, the page of the Duke of Savoy.

COMTE FRANCESCO MARAVIGLIA, her father.

LA COMTESSE MARAVIGLIA.

COMTE ODOARDO MARAVIGLIA, Leona's brother, Ambassador of the Kings of France and Spain.

JOHN FREDERICK, Elector of Saxony.

ADMIRAL OF CASTILE,
DUKE OF MEDINA COELI,
RUY GOMEZ DE SILVA, } Spanish noblemen.
DUKE OF ALVA,
DON LUIS DE VARGAS,

FRANCESCO MARIA SFORZA, Duke of Milan.
ARCHBISHOP OF TOLEDO.
CARDINAL POLE.
WILLIAM OF ORANGE.
DON GUZMAN D'AVILA, Herald of Spain.
SIGNOR ANGELO POLICASTRO, Astrologer to Charles V.
COMTE WALDECK, in the cavalry service of Charles V.
VICOMTE WALDECK, his son.
THE BASTARD SON OF COMTE WALDECK.
ODINET DE MONTFORT, a Savoyard cavalier.
COUNCILLOR PHILIBERT BRUSSELIUS.
FRANÇOIS I., King of France.
HENRI II., his successor.
CATHERINE DE MÉDICIS,
DIANE DE POITIERS.
DIANE DE CASTRO.
MARGUERITE DE FRANCE, sister of Henri II.
THE DAUPHIN, afterwards François II.
MARY STUART, married to the Dauphin.
MARY FLEMING,
MARY SEATON,
MARY LIVINGSTON,
MARY BEATON, } Mary Stuart's "Four Marys."
ELIZABETH DE VALOIS,
MARGUERITE DE VALOIS, } daughters of Henri II.
DUC D'ORLÉANS, afterwards Charles IX.
DUC DE NEVERS, Lieutenant-general of the king.
HENRI, his brother, afterwards Henri III.
CONSTABLE DE MONTMORENCY.
GABRIEL DE MONTMORENCY, his son.
MONSIEUR DE CHATILLON, the Constable's nephew.
FRANÇOIS, Duc de Guise.
CARDINAL DE LORRAINE,
DUC D'AUMALE,
MARQUIS D'ELBŒUF,
CARDINAL GUISE. } his brothers.

ADMIRAL COLIGNY, Envoy extraordinary of Henri II.
MONSIEUR DANDELOT DE COLIGNY, his brother.
MONSIEUR DE BOISSY, Grand Equerry of France.
MONSIEUR DE VIEILLEVILLE, Grand Chamberlain.
ALPHONSE D'ESTE, Duc de Ferrara.
DUCHESSE DE NEMOURS.
CARDINAL CARAFFA.
GABRIEL DE LORGES.
AMBROISE PARÉ,
ANDREW VESALIUS, } surgeons.
RONSARD,
RÉMY BELLEAU,
DORAT,
DU BELLAY, } men of letters at the French Court.
JACQUES AMYOT,
M. DANESIUS, } preceptors of the princes.
JACQUES DE LA MOTTE, Abbé de St. Prix.
DUC D'ENGHIEN,
MARÉCHAL DE SAINT-ANDRÉ,
DUC DE NEVERS,
MARÉCHAL STROZZI,
MARÉCHAL DE BRISSAC,
MONSIEUR DE THÉLIGNY,
MONSIEUR DE BREUIL,
MONSIEUR DE JARNAC,
CAPTAIN LANGUETOT,
CAPTAIN RAMBOUILLET, } French officers.
CAPTAIN LOUIS POY,
MONSIEUR DANDELOT, the admiral's brother,
VICOMTE DU MONT NOTRE-DAME,
SIEUR DE LA CURÉE,
COMTE DE LA ROCHEFOUCAULD,
DUC DE MONTPENSIER,
DUC DE LONGUEVILLE,
DUC DE BOUILLON,
VICOMTE DE TURENNE,

HEINRICH SCHARFENSTEIN,
MARTIN PILLETROUSE,
FRANTZ SCHARFENSTEIN,
CÆSAR ANNIBAL MALEMORT,
HONORÉ-JOSEPH MALDENT,
JEAN-CHRYSOSTOME PROCOPE,
VICTOR-FELIX YVONNET,
CYRILLE-NEPOMUCÈNE LACTANCE,
VITTORIO-ALBANI FRACASSO,
} soldiers of fortune in the French service.

COUNT EGMONT,
COUNT HORN,
COUNT SCHWARZBOURG,
COUNT MANSFIELD,
DUKE ERIC OF BRUNSWICK,
DUKE ERNEST OF BRUNSWICK,
FIELD-MARSHAL DE BINNSCOURT,
CAPTAIN CARONDELET,
COLONEL NARVAEZ,
JULIAN ROMERON,
ALONZO DE CAZIÈRES,
} officers in the army besieging St. Quentin.

MADEMOISELLE GERTRUDE,
PHILIPPIN,
} servants at the Château du Parcq.

JEAN PAUQUET, captain of a company at St. Quentin.
GUILLAUME PAUQUET, his brother.
GUDULE, Guillaume Pauquet's daughter.
MAITRE GOSSEU, a Picard peasant.
CATHERINE, his wife.

MARGUERITE DE VALOIS.

INTRODUCTORY NOTE.

THE series of romances in which Dumas has dealt
with the courts of the later Valois kings, Charles
IX. and Henri III., — a series of which " La Reine
Margot," or "Marguerite de Valois," is the first
chronologically speaking, — describes the main
events of the period with such substantial accuracy
that one who reads this great trilogy may be fairly
said to be studying French history, if not perhaps
preparing himself to write it.

From the death of Henri II. through the reigns
of the three sons of that unhappy monarch, — the
sickly and ill-fated François II., the cruel, almost
insane, Charles IX., and the effeminate, irresolute,
and cowardly Henri III., — the one pervading personality in France was that of Catherine de Médicis;
and as her hatred and fear of Henri of Navarre
was the mainspring of her policy from the time
that his character became so developed as to distin-
guish him from the other princes of the Bourbon
family, all of whom were adherents of the re-

formed religion, and to attract to him the warm
and enthusiastic devotion of the constantly increas-
ing Huguenot party, so has Dumas taken that
hatred and that fear for the theme upon which he
has constructed three romances which rival, in intense interest and power to entertain and amuse,
any that have ever come even from his pen.

If it was from the lips of Charles that the order
for the bloody work of St. Bartholomew's Day,
1572, issued, it was the mind of the queen mother
that prompted it, and the will of the queen mother
that forced it from those lips; and the vast numbers of Huguenots that were massacred in the
streets of Paris in pursuance of that order were
sacrificed pitilessly and ruthlessly in the hope that
in the general carnage the king of Navarre would
be put out of the way with his co-religionists.

The assassination of Gaspard de Coligny, the
brave Admiral, whose services to France had been
so great, can never cease to be an event of sad and
mournful interest to all lovers of religious liberty;
and the vivid description of the foul deed to be
found in the following pages derives added interest
from the fact that the part therein assigned to
Coconnas was really performed by him.

M. De Crue has recently published in Paris a
book entitled, *"Le Parti des Politiques au lendemain*

de la Saint-Barthélemy," and which has for its sub-title, *"La Molle et Coconat,"* which it seems is in each instance the more authentic orthography.

It appears from the researches of M. de Crue that our two heroes were even more important person-ages than they are represented by Dumas to have been. The party of the *Politiques* occupied a sort of middle position between the Catholics and Huguenots; it was originally headed by the Mont-morencys, and after them by François, Duc d'Alen-çon. La Molle, described as dissolute, pious, very superstitious, became the confidant of d'Alençon; and it is said that Charles IX., who detested his brother, twice gave the order to strangle La Molle; and that one day he himself, with the Duc de Guise and other gentlemen, waited in a passage at the Louvre for that purpose. La Molle was saved only because he entered the room of the Queen of Navarre instead of d'Alençon's.

Annibal Coconat (or Coconata) is said by M. De Crue to have been taken as an associate by La Molle to supply personal courage, in which he was lacking. They were both secret agents of Spain, which power was under Philip II. always industriously fomenting the religious troubles in France. Charles IX. is quoted as having spoken of Coconat thus: "Coconat was a valiant gentleman.

but he was wicked; he was one of the wickedest
men living in my kingdom. I remember having
heard him say, among other things, when he vaunted
his part in the Saint Bartholomew, that he had
bought from the hands of the people thirty Huguenots in order to have the satisfaction of killing
them after his own pleasure, which was, first to
make them renounce their religion with a promise
to save their lives; this being done, he killed them
with his poniard cruelly with several cuts."

This monarch, who was horrified at such "wickedness" and "cruelty," is the same who stood at
the window of the Louvre on the same occasion,
shooting at passing Huguenots with his arquebus.

In 1574 a scheme was formed (by La Molle ?)
which provided that d'Alençon was to fly from
Paris with the King of Navarre, Turenne, and
Coconat, and put himself at the head of all the
malcontents of the kingdom, the expectation being
that Ludwig of Nassau and his army would support
him, as well as England, Germany, and the Netherlands. The spies of the queen mother, however,
ferreted out the plot. D'Alençon and the King of
Navarre were kept prisoners in the Louvre, while
La Molle and Coconat were arrested. The first was
looked upon as the head of the conspiracy, Coconat
merely as an instrument. They were both put to

the torture. La Molle, after keeping silent for a long while, finally denounced as his accomplices Turenne, Coconat, Bouillon, Condé, and others, but did not breathe the name of D'Alençon. Coconat, however, did speak, under torture, of D'Alençon and Montmorency.

La Molle was the lover of the Queen of Navarre; – the Duchesse de Nevers was one of Coconat's many mistresses. Marguerite pleaded for La Molle's pardon, but could only obtain a promise that he should not have a public execution; but the preparations were hastened, and before the order arrived they were both beheaded in the Place de Grève.

Brautôme says that Marguerite and the Duchesse de Nevers secretly disinterred the bodies, and had them buried in the Chapel of Saint Martin at Montmartre. It was said also that they kept the heads of their lovers embalmed.

A poet of the time composed this epigram for La Molle: "*Mollis vita fuit, mollior interitus.*"

This brief sketch of the results of historical research will enable the reader to judge for himself how closely Dumas has adhered to fact.

History has had much to say of Marguerite de Valois, Queen of Navarre, — of her fatal beauty and her even more fatal levity of character, to call it by no harsher name. Dumas has certainly presented her to us here in quite as favorable a light as the known facts of her life and character warrant. Our own historian, Motley, has had a word to say of her when telling the story of her brother François's brief experience as Governor-General of the Netherlands. Her relations with that brother have been commented upon very severely; she accompanied him to the Netherlands, where she added many names to the list of those whom her charms had seduced, — notably that of Don John of Austria, the hero of Lepanto.

It would be difficult, indeed, to imagine a tale otherwise than interesting which should have for its central figure, or for one of its central figures, the jovial, *insouciant*, captivating, lovable, but withal shrewd and calculating, Henri de Bourbon, King of Navarre, afterwards Henri IV. of France. Always present, a gay and mocking spectre in the minds of Catherine de Médicis and her childless sons, unstable in love and in religion, but always manly and brave, generous and loyal, the son of Jeanne d'Albret is the true hero of the Valois Romances.

MARGUERITE DE VALOIS.

LIST OF CHARACTERS.

Period, 1572-1575.

CHARLES IX., King of France.

HENRI, Duc d'Anjou, } his brothers.
FRANÇOIS, Duc d'Alençon, }

CATHERINE DE MÉDICIS, the Queen Mother.

ELIZABETH, Queen to Charles IX.

HENRI DE BOURBON, King of Navarre, afterwards Henri IV.

MARGUERITE DE VALOIS, his wife.

PRINCESS CLAUDE, Duchesse de Lorraine, sister of Marguerite de Valois.

MARIE TOUCHET, mistress of Charles IX.

CHARLES, their infant son, afterwards Duc d'Angoulême.

HENRI DE LORRAINE, Duc de Guise.

DUCHESSE DE NEVERS, his sister-in-law.

BARON DE SAUVE.

MADAME DE SAUVE, his wife, lady-in-waiting to Catherine de Médicis.

MADEMOISELLE DARIOLE, her waiting-woman.

GILONNE, daughter of Marshal de Matignon, and confidante of Marguerite de Valois.

MADELON, the old nurse of Charles IX.

COMTE JOSEPH HYACINTHE BONIFACE DE LERAC DE LA MOLE, a Huguenot, beloved by Marguerite de Valois.

COMTE ANNIBAL DE COCONNAS, a Catholic, beloved by the Duchesse de Nevers.

MAÎTRE CABOUCHE, headsman to the provostry of Paris.

FRANÇOIS DE LOUVIERS-MAUREVEL, " the King's Killer."

MAÎTRE RENÉ, Florentine, "perfumer to her Majesty the Queen Mother."

AMBROISE PARÉ, surgeon.

M. DE NANCEY, Captain of the Guards to Catherine de Médicis.

MAÎTRE LA HURIÈRE, a Catholic, landlord of the Belle Étoile Inn.

GRÉGOIRE, his servant.

MADAME LA HURIÈRE.

M. DE BESME, a German officer, and adherent to the Duc de Guise.

ORTHON, page to Henry of Navarre.

M. DE BEAULIEU, Governor of Vincennes.

CAPTAIN LA CHASTRO, of the King's Guards.

BISHOP OF CRACOW, } Ambassadors from Poland.
THE PALATINE LASCO,

ADMIRAL DE COLIGNY,
PRINCE DE CONDÉ,
M. DE TÉLIGNY,
M. DE MOUY. DE SAINT-PHALE,
M. DE SANCOURT,   } Huguenots.
M. DE BARTHÉLEMY,
LAMBERT MERCANDON,
OLIVIER, his son.
MADAME DE MERCANDON,

LE PROCUREUR-GÉNÉRAL.

PRESIDENT OF THE COURT AT VINCENNES.

CLERK OF THE COURT.

MAZILLE, a physician.

LA DAME DE MONSOREAU.

INTRODUCTORY NOTE.

In "La Dame de Monsoreau," we find Henri III., the third son of Henri II., occupying the throne of France. He it was who, as Duc d'Anjou, was chosen King of Poland, — as related in "Marguerite de Valois," — and who returned to Paris so opportunely as Charles IX. was breathing his last, summoned by Catherine de Médicis, whose favorite son he was. We find him, last and weakest of the Valois, surrounded and ruled by unworthy favorites, the famous "Mignons;" and much less king in fact than any one of half a dozen others.

The Catholic League has grown in numbers and in audacity, and the Guises find a willing tool in the king's brother, François, Duc d'Anjou, formerly Duc d'Alençon, now, as always, ready to commit any treachery and enter into any agreement which looks to the placing of a crown on his head.

The various scenes in the Abbey of Sainte-Geneviève will be to many readers among the most engrossing, from their historical interest as well as from the prominent part taken in them

by the inimitable Chicot, the court "jester." If
Dumas had done nothing else to earn our gratitude,
it would certainly be due to him in large measure
for enabling us to make the acquaintance of Chicot,
whose "jesting" served his master far better than
the selfish devotion of all his "Mignons." Never
was a character in history or romance farther removed from the common conception of a court
fool; and while he is responsible for some of the
most amusing and entertaining chapters that were
ever written, he takes no step, indeed scarce utters
a word, which has not a definite purpose connected
with the interests of the king, whose only true
friend he seems to be; while at the same time
he sees him as he is, in all his weakness and
effeminacy, and estimates him at his true value.
Whether he is engaged in drinking Gorenflot under
the table, belaboring the Duc de Mayenne while
he vainly struggles to crawl through a hole too
small for his famous paunch, or fighting his other
old enemy, the lawyer Nicolas David, to the death,
he is always the same Chicot, — cool, shrewd, per-
fectly self-possessed, brave as a lion, and with an
inexhaustible store of good-humored persiflage and
biting wit.

"The passions in your tales," says Andrew Lang,
in "Letters to Dead Authors," "are honorable and

brave; the motives are clearly human. Honor, love, friendship make the threefold clew your knights and dames follow through how delightful a labyrinth of adventures!"

How fitly do these words apply to those portions of "La Dame de Monsoreau" which are concerned with the passion aroused by Diane de Méridor in the heart of that hero of heroes, Comte Louis de Clermont, called Bussy d'Amboise, and with the fatal result of that passion, contributed to by the jealousy of Monsoreau, the cowardice of d'Épernon, and the inborn, motiveless wickedness of that most contemptible of all characters in French history, François de Valois, Duc d'Anjou!

The heroic defence of Bussy d'Amboise against the combined attack of Monsoreau and his band of ruffians and the cut-throats in the pay of d'Épernon long ago took its place at the head of the master-pieces of description in its kind.

Says Mr. Lang, in the same letter quoted from above: "I know four good fights of one against a multitude in literature. These are the Death of Gretir the Strong, the Death of Gunnar of Lithend, the Death of Hereward the Wake, and the Death of Bussy d'Amboise. We can compare the strokes of the heroic fighting times with those described in later days; and upon my word, I do not know that

the short sword of Gretir or the bill of Skarphedin
or the bow of Gunnar was better wielded than the
rapier of your Bussy or the sword and shield of
Hereward."

But in our admiration of the magnificent swordsmanship, the superb coolness, and the heroic courage
of the central figure, we must not overlook the
other elements which add to the power of the
description and the tense and thrilling interest of
the scene, — on the one hand, the unselfish devotion
of Rémy and the heart-broken despair of Diane ;
on the other hand, the cold-blooded heartlessness
and cynicism of d'Anjou, the real instigator of the
plot against his popular and powerful — indeed, too
powerful — follower.

Diane lived ! Her love for Bussy d'Amboise was
the undying passion of a noble-hearted woman who
loves but once ; she lived to avenge the murder of
her lover upon the head of the royal assassin.   In
" The Forty-Five," the third and last of the Valois
cycle of romances, Dumas has followed and described the course of her vengeance to its fearful
end.

LA DAME DE MONSOREAU.

LIST OF CHARACTERS.

Period, 1578.

HENRI III., King of France.
FRANÇOIS, Duc d'Anjou, his brother, formerly Duc d'Alençon.
AURILLY, a lute-player, the confidant of Duc d'Anjou.
LOUISE DE LORRAINE, wife of Henri III.
CATHERINE DE MÉDICIS, the Queen Mother.
CHICOT, the King's jester, a Gascon gentleman.
HENRI DE BOURBON, King of Navarre.
MADEMOISELLE DE MONTMORENCY, "la Fosseuse," his mistress
M. AGRIPPA D'AUBIGNÉ, his friend.
COMTE LOUIS DE CLERMONT, called Bussy d'Amboise.
M. CHARLES BALZAC D'ANTRAGUES, } friends of Bussy
FRANÇOIS D'AUDIE, Vicomte de Ribeirac, } d'Amboise.
M. DE LIVAROT, }
FRANÇOIS D'ÉPINAY DE SAINT-LUC, favorite of Henri III.
JEANNE DE COSSÉ, his wife.
MARÉCHAL DE BRISSAC, her father.
M. BRYAN DE MONSOREAU, chief huntsman.
DIANE DE MÉRIDOR, his wife, "La Dame de Monsoreau," in
    love with Bussy d'Amboise.
BARON DE MÉRIDOR, Diane's father.
RÉMY LE HAUDOUIN, a young surgeon.
GERTRUDE, Diane's servant.
M. D'ÉPERNON, }
M. DE SCHOMBERG, } friends of the king.
M. DE MAUGIRON, }
JACQUES DE LEVIS, Comte de Quélus, }

M. DE CRILLON, an officer of the king.
HENRI, Duc de Guise,
CARDINAL DE LORRAINE,
DUC DE MAYENNE,
DUCHESSE DE MONTPENSIER, his sister,
MAÎTRE NICOLAS DAVID, an advocate,
M. PIERRE DE GONDY,
M. LE GOUVERNEUR D'AUNIS,
M. DE CASTILLON,
BARON DE LUSIGNAN,
M. CRUCÉ,
M. LECLERC,

} Leaguers, conspiring against Henri III.

CHANCELLOR DE MORVILLIERS.
M. DE NANCEY, Captain of the Guards.
JOSEPH FOULON, superior of the Convent of Sainte Geneviève.
CLAUDE BONHOMET, host of the " Corne d'Abondance."
M. BERNOUILLET, of the hostelry of La Croix.
MAÎTRE LA HURIÈRE, of the Belle Étoile Inn.
BROTHER GORENFLOT.

THE FORTY-FIVE.

INTRODUCTORY NOTE.

SOME six or seven years elapsed between the tragical death of Bussy d'Amboise, as told in the concluding chapters of "La Dame de Monsoreau," and the coming to Paris of the famous Gascon body-guard of Henri III., known in history as the Forty-Five, with which this tale opens.

The vengeance wrought by Diane de Méridor upon the prince, who was the instigator of the concerted attack upon Bussy, is the theme from which the "Forty-Five" derives most of its romantic interest. Diane, the lovely, lovable, loving woman, has become a cold, loveless, pitiless statue, living only to avenge her murdered lover; but she is still beautiful, almost superhumanly beautiful, — so beautiful that Henri de Joyeuse is lost in hopeless love of her, and that the perfidious Duc d'Anjou, the object of her relentless pursuit, thirsts to possess her, and by his very passion makes her

task easy. History records that he died, from an
unexplained cause, at Château-Thierry on the date
here assigned.

The acquaintance so pleasantly begun in the
earlier story, with Chicot, is here renewed with
even greater delight. Disguised as Maître Robert
Briquet, to escape the vengeance of the Duc de
Mayenne, he is no less original and amusing than
in his proper person, — no less active in his care for
the interests of the somewhat unappreciative and
ungrateful master, to whom his faithful attachment
never varies.

The whole episode of the jester's mission to the
Court of Navarre — his hazardous journey, his brief
stay at Nerac, the "hunt" which ended at Cahors,
and his narration of his experiences to the king on
his return — would alone be sufficient to stamp the
"Forty-Five" as one of the very best of our author's
romances. In all his varied experiences, Chicot
never found his match in shrewdness and finesse
till he crossed swords with Henri of Navarre. And
how frankly he acknowledged his defeat, and how
warmly each appreciated the other's merits!

The events which led to the journey of the Duc
d'Anjou to Flanders with the hope of wearing a

crown at last, the course of William of Orange towards the French prince, and the abortive attempt upon Antwerp, are sufficiently touched upon in the body of the story. François, after all his longing and scheming, died uncrowned; and it may be doubted whether he would ever have ascended the French throne, even if he had outlived his brother. Had he done so, it is safe to say that the crimes and shortcomings of his brothers would have been almost forgotten, and the odium which attaches to the memory of the last degenerate Valois kings would have been concentrated upon him.

The constant growth of the Holy League under the leadership of the Guises, and with the almost avowed patronage of Philip II. of Spain, is interestingly woven into the narrative; perhaps we need not marvel at the success of a cause which had for its high priestess so charming a personality as the heroine of the celebrated golden scissors, — that energetic *intrigante*, the clever and fascinating Duchesse de Montpensier.

It is interesting to know the estimation in which these romances were held by their author's compatriot, George Sand, herself a novelist of the first rank.

Says Andrew Lang in his "Essays in Little:"
"M. Borie chanced to visit the famous novelist just
before her death, and found Dumas's novel, 'Les
Quarante-Cinq,' lying on her table. He expressed
his wonder that she was reading it for the first
time. 'For the first time!' said she; 'why, this is
the fifth or sixth time I have read "Les Quarante-
Cinq" and the others. When I am ill, anxious,
melancholy, tired, discouraged, nothing helps me
against moral and physical troubles like a book of
Dumas.'"

THE FORTY-FIVE.

LIST OF CHARACTERS.

Period, 1585.

HENRI III., King of France.

LOUISE DE LORRAINE, his wife.

FRANÇOIS, Duc d'Anjou, brother of Henri III.

AURILLY, the confidant of Duc d'Anjou.

CATHERINE DE MÉDICIS, the Queen Mother.

CHICOT, the King's jester, passing under the name of Robert Briquet.

ANNE, Duc de Joyeuse, Grand Admiral of France.

HENRI DE JOYEUSE, Comte du Bouchage, } his brothers
FRANÇOIS, Cardinal de Joyeuse,

NOGARET DE LAVALETTE, Duc d'Épernon.

COMTE DE SAINT-AIGNAN.

M. DE LOIGNAC, Captain of the Forty-Five Guardsmen.

VICOMTE ERNAUTON DE CARMAINGES,
M. DE SAINTE-MALINE,
M. DE CHALABRE,
PERCUDAS DE PINCORNAY,   } of the "Forty-Five."
PERTINAX DE MONTCRABEAU,
EUSTACHE DE MIRADOUX,
HECTOR DE BIRAN,

M. DE CRILLON, Colonel of the French Guards.

M. DE VESIN, commanding the garrison at Cahors.

DIANE DE MÉRIDOR.

RÉMY LE HAUDOUIN.

THE SUPERIOR OF THE CONVENT OF THE HOSPITALIÈRES.

HENRI, Duc de Guise,
DUC DE MAYENNE,
DUCHESSE DE MONTPENSIER, his sister,
M. DE MAYNEVILLE,
M. DE CRUCÉ,
BUSSY-LECLERC,
M. DE MARTEAU,
NICOLAS POULAIN, lieutenant to the
provost of Paris,
} Leaguers.

PRESIDENT BRISSON OF THE COUNCIL.
M. DE SALCÈDE.
HENRI DE BOURBON, King of Navarre.
MARGUERITE, his wife.
M. DE TURENNE,
M. D'AUBIAC,
M. DUPLESSIS-DE MORNAY,
} of the Court of Navarre.

MADEMOISELLE DE MONTMORENCY, " la Fosseuse," mistress of
the King of Navarre.
WILLIAM OF NASSAU, Prince of Orange.
THE BURGOMASTER OF ANTWERP.
GOES, a Flemish sailor.
DOM MODESTE GORENFLOT,
BROTHER EUSÈBE,
BROTHER JACQUES,
BROTHER BORROMÉE,
BROTHER PANURGE,
} of the Priory of the Jacobins.

MAÎTRE BONHOMET, host of the " Corne d'Abondance" inn.
MAÎTRE FOURNICHON, host of " The Sword of the Brave Cheva-
lier."
DAME FOURNICHON, his wife.
LARDILLE DE CHAVANTRADE, wife of Eustache de Miradoux.
MILITOR DE CHAVANTRADE, her son.
MAÎTRE MITON,
JEAN FRIARD,
} bourgeois.

MIRON, a Physician.

THE THREE MUSKETEERS

INTRODUCTORY NOTE.

No other one of all the works of the elder Dumas, with the possible exception of "Monte Cristo," is so widely known and read, and so universally popular among English-speaking people, as that which relates the thrilling adventures of the "Three Musketeers" and their friend and brother, the clever Gascon, D'Artagnan, who has held, for many years, an undisputed place in the very front rank of heroes of romance. In many countries and languages, and upon the stage, the bravery and wit of the four inseparables have enthralled and fascinated more than one generation; and countless readers yet to come will find enjoyment in the most striking exemplification of the marvellous story-telling powers of the great writer, of whom a favorite essayist of our own day has said: "The past and present are photographed imperishably on his brain; he knows the manners of all ages and all countries, the names of all the arms that men have used, all the garments they have worn, all the dishes they have tasted, all the terms of all professions from swordsmanship to coach-building."

Those readers who find a never-failing source of
enjoyment in what Macaulay might have called
the *audacia Gasconica* of D'Artagnan, and in the
simple-hearted, good-humored, unquestioning loy-
alty of Porthos, the Titan; who never tire of
travelling with the famous four from Paris to
London to save the honor of Anne of Austria;
who follow with bated breath the gradual perver-
sion and corruption by Milady of the Puritan
Felton, and shudder at the vengeance wreaked
upon her by those to whom her hideous crimes
have brought unhappiness and suffering, — all such
may take comfort in the assurance that every painful or pleasurable emotion they feel has been felt
and acknowledged by those whose judgment in
matters literary we love to respect. The list is a
long one of eminent writers who have borne testimony to the enjoyment they have taken in the
doughty deeds of the heroes of these volumes.

"Think of a whole day in bed and a good novel
for a companion!" says Thackeray, in his "Roundabout Papers." "The Chevalier d'Artagnan to tell
me stories from dawn to night! . . . Suppose
Athos, Porthos, and Aramis should enter with a
noiseless swagger, curling their mustaches. . . . Of
your heroic heroes, I think Monseigneur Athos,
Count de la Fère, is my favorite. I have read
about him from sunrise to sunset with the utmost
contentment of mind. He has passed through how

many volumes? Forty? Fifty? I wish, for my
part, there were a hundred more, and would never
tire of him rescuing prisoners, punishing ruffians,
and running scoundrels through the midriff with
his most graceful rapier. Ah, Athos, Porthos, and
Aramis, you are a magnificent trio!"

Robert Louis Stevenson and Hayward, the clever
essayist, have put themselves, unhesitatingly, on
record as ardent admirers of Dumas and his chivalrous heroes; and Andrew Lang surrenders to the
charm quite as completely, and in his most graceful manner, in one of his "Letters to Dead
Authors."

"You gave us," he writes, "the valor of
D'Artagnan, the strength of Porthos, the melancholy nobility of Athos: Honor, Chivalry, and
Friendship. I declare your characters are real
people to me, and old friends. . . . The reproach of
being amusing has somewhat dimmed your fame
for a moment. The shadow of this tyranny will
soon be overpast, and men and women — and above
all, boys — will laugh and weep over the page of
Alexandre Dumas. Like Scott himself, you take
us captive in our childhood. I remember a very
idle little boy who was busy with the 'Three
Musketeers' when he should have been occupied
with 'Wilkins's Latin Prose.' 'Twenty years after'
(alas! and more) he is still constant to that gallant
company, and at this very moment is breathlessly

wondering whether Grimaud will steal M. de Beaufort out of the Cardinal's prison."

It may be said of this and of the other volumes of the group in which D'Artagnan is a principal figure, as indeed it may be said of all the historical tales of this incomparable writer, that the interest is greatly intensified by the knowledge that in all the main features, as well as in many details, the narrative deals with well-vouched historical facts, and with personages who have actually existed, and whose portraits are generally drawn with great faithfulness.

The leading motive of this tale, Cardinal Richelieu's bitter enmity to Anne of Austria and to her bosom-friend and confidante, Madame de Chevreuse, is a well-authenticated fact. The same is true of the king's lack of affection for his wife, which originated in her apparent partiality for his brother Gaston, who was at first known as Duc d'Anjou, afterwards as Duc d'Orléans, and was the father of "La Grande Mademoiselle." The disappointment of Louis XIII. at the queen's long-continued sterility contributed to alienate his affection from her; but the powerful influence of the king's master, the omnipotent cardinal, was the principal factor in keeping the husband and wife apart.

Richelieu's hatred for the young queen dated from an early period after her arrival in France, — when the queen mother, Marie de Médicis, although somewhat discredited, was still a power to be reckoned with, and in the event of the king's death without issue, would again become regent during the minority of Gaston, a contingency equally to be dreaded by the queen and the cardinal. Louis was ill, how ill no one knew; and the cardinal determined on a bold stroke. He arrayed himself in the costume of a cavalier — he was then young and handsome — and paid a visit to Anne of Austria one evening at the hour when her ladies generally left her alone; he desired to speak with her, so he said, on affairs of State. Unattended except by her old Spanish maid, she received him graciously, and was at once informed by him that his real purpose was to speak of her own affairs.

He told her that the king was seriously ill, that his physician had told him that, although death was not imminent, he could never recover; and he thereupon forcibly impressed upon her how deplorable would be her situation if the king should die without an heir of his body.

She was painfully surprised, but replied to his representations that their fate was in God's hands, and nothing more was to be said.

"Yes," said the cardinal, smiling; "but God said to his creatures: 'Help yourself and heaven will help you.'"

Being pressed by the queen to divulge his real meaning, he finally did so, and avowed his love for her as a justification for the audacious proposals he dared to make. The queen "dissembled her contempt, and determined to see how far the cardinal's passion would carry him."

She demanded time for reflection, and made an appointment with him for the next night; and in the meantime, in concert with Madame de Chevreuse, concocted a scheme to make him ridiculous. When he appeared the next night, the queen said that she desired to put his affection to the proof, and therefore demanded that he should dance a saraband for her in the costume of a Spanish buffoon. To her surprise he at once consented, on condition that she should be the only spectator, and that the music should be furnished by a retainer of his own.

The following night, Madame de Chevreuse, Vauthier, and Beringhen were carefully stowed away behind a screen. The violinist appeared, followed shortly by the cardinal himself, arrayed in green velvet breeches and doublet, with silver bells at his knees and castanets in his hands.

At a gesture from the queen, " he began to perform the saraband, capering about the room and waving his arms in due form. Unluckily, the very seriousness with which the cardinal went about it was so absurd to look upon that the queen could not keep a sober face, and burst out laughing. A prolonged shriek of laughter came from behind the screen, like an echo of hers. The cardinal saw that what he

had taken for a special favor was only a practical
joke, and he left the room in a furious rage. . . .
Poor fools they were to play thus with the cardinal-
duke's wrath! To be sure, that wrath was still an
unknown quantity. After the death of Bouteville,
Montmorency, Chalais, and Cinq-Mars, they certainly would not have risked such a dangerous
pleasantry.

"While they were laughing at its success the
cardinal was vowing everlasting hatred to Anne of
Austria and Madame de Chevreuse."

When the Duke of Buckingham, the magnificent
and accomplished courtier and favorite of Charles
I., came to the French court as negotiator of the
projected alliance between Charles, then Prince of
Wales, and the king's sister, Henrietta Maria, he
fell at once a victim to the charms of the queen,
and made no secret of his infatuation. The jealous
hatred of the cardinal was quick to seize this means
of annoying the woman who had so deeply wounded
his self-esteem. His emissaries watched every movement of the queen and the ambassador, and by his
means devices of all sorts were resorted to, and
traps laid to dishonor her. As the difficulties in
the way of meeting the object of his affections,
except by stealth, became greater, the duke's expe-
dients to overcome them became ever more daring
and foolhardy, and in all of them he found a zealous coadjutor in Madame de Chevreuse, — "lovely,

clever, and audacious, ... ready to enter heart and soul into any intrigue, no matter how whimsical or hare-brained."

The duke prolonged the negotiations for the marriage as long as he could, and when at last he was obliged to leave France with the new queen of England, he used all his power to obtain a permanent appointment as ambassador to Louis XIII.

"He set fire to two great kingdoms," says one chronicler, "staking the future of England, whose ruin he nearly compassed, and his own life, which he finally lost, against the chance of remaining in France as ambassador, in order to be near Anne of Austria, in spite of the inflexible determination of Richelieu."

The episode of the diamond studs, in which D'Artagnan's passion for Madame Bonacieux leads to our heroes' playing so prominent a part, actually occurred, substantially as here related: the queen bestowed the jewels upon the infatuated duke; the snare was laid by the cardinal, and Buckingham gave a most convincing proof of his devotion when he put an embargo upon all the ports of England while his own jeweller was making fac-similes to replace two of the pendants which had been cut off by "Milady Clarik."

It is equally true that the murderous deed of the fanatic Felton occurred at a moment most opportunely chosen to serve the ends of Louis XIII.,

— that is to say, of Richelieu. The joy of both at the death of the duke was exuberant and openly expressed; and Anne of Austria believed, to her dying day, that her relentless foe inspired the deed.

A short time before the tragic death of Buckingham, Richelieu had dealt a deadly blow at the queen's credit, and had struck dismay into the hearts of all his enemies by his characteristically clever manipulation of the conspiracy of Chalais, in which Gaston d'Orléans and the two illegitimate sons of Henri IV. by Gabriel d'Estrées were involved. By promising clemency to Chalais, he forced from him a confession, in which he denounced the queen and Gaston as parties to a plot to assassinate king and cardinal, and to marry one another. The results of this affair were the disgrace of the queen, the unwilling marriage of Gaston to Mademoiselle de Guise, and the exile of Madame de Chevreuse, whose stolen visits to Paris and correspondence with Aramis under the name of Marie Michon form one of the brightest episodes in the "Three Musketeers."

In the succeeding volumes of this cycle, the reader will fall in again with the Gascon and his tried and true friends, and follow their fortunes through stirring and troublous times, when they had become to some extent involved in the political movements of the period; but will never find them more attractive or more diverting than in the early days of their defensive and offensive alliance, when they thought no more of casting defiance in the teeth of the great cardinal himself than of breakfasting in the bastion of Saint-Gervais, under the guns of Rochelle, to win a wager, — when, in short, they made for themselves the reputation for dauntless courage, invincible prowess, and chivalrous gallantry which passed into a tradition at the French court.

THE THREE MUSKETEERS.

LIST OF CHARACTERS.

Period, 1626–1628.

Louis XIII., King of France.
Anne of Austria, his wife.
Armand Jean Duplessis, Cardinal Richelieu, Minister of State.
George Villiers, Duke of Buckingham.
Patrick, his confidential servant.
M. de Tréville, Captain of the King's Musketeers.
Duc de la Trémouille, commanding the Cardinal's Guards.
D'Artagnan, a Gascon adventurer, afterwards lieutenant in the King's Musketeers.

Athos,
Porthos,
Aramis, } the "Three Musketeers," serving under M. de Tréville.

Comte de Rochefort,
Comte de Wardes,
Lady de Winter, } in the service of Richelieu.

Duchesse de Chevreuse, the friend of Anne of Austria.

M. le Comte de Soissons,
Duc d'Elboeuf,
Comte d'Harcourt,
M. de Baradas,
Duc de Longueville,
Comte de la Roche-Guyon,
Comte de Cramail,
Chevalier de Souveray,
M. de Liancourt. } of the French Court.

M. DE SÉGUIER, keeper of the Seals.

M. DE BASSOMPIERRE,
M. DE SCHOMBERG,   French officers at 'the Siege of
DUC D'ANGOULÊME,   Rochelle.
M. DE TOIRAS,

LA CHESNAYE, confidential valet of Louis XIII.

DONNA ESTEFANIA, the Spanish confidant of Anne of Austria.

M. LAPORTE, the queen's servant.

MADAME DE GUITAUT,
MADAME DE SABLÉ,
MADAME DE MONTBAZON,   in attendance on Anne of Austria.
MADAME DE GUÉMÉNÉE,

MADAME DE SURGIS,   spies of Richelieu, attending on Anne
MADAME DE LANNOY,   of Austria.

JACQUES MICHEL BONACIEUX.

CONSTANCE, his wife, in love with D'Artagnan.

M. COQUENARD, procurator.

MADAME COQUENARD, in love with Porthos.

GRIMAUD, servant to Athos.

MOUSQUETON, Porthos's servant.

BAZIN, servant to Aramis.

PLANCHET, D'Artagnan's servant.

M. D'ESSART, brother-in-law of M. de Tréville, commanding a
    company of the King's Guards.

SIEUR DE LA COSTE, an ensign in the King's Guards.

M. DE MONTARAN, of the Musketeers.

M. DUHALLIER, commanding a company of guards.

M. DE BUSIGNY, of the light horse.

M. DE CAVOIS,   captains in the Cardinal's Guards.
LA HOUDINIÈRE,

M. DE JUSSAC,
M. DE CAHUSAC,
M. DE BICARAT,   of the Cardinal's Guards.
M. DE BERNAJOUX,

VITRAY, a messenger of Cardinal Richelieu.

LUBIN, lackey of Comte de Wardes.

BRISEMONT, a soldier.

FOUBREAU, a lackey.

GODEAU, Purveyor of the Musketeers.

THE EXECUTIONER OF LILLE.

THE SUPERIOR OF THE CARMELITE CONVENT AT BÉTHUNE.

THE CURATE OF MONTDIDIER.

THE PRINCIPAL OF AMIENS, superior of the Jesuits.

M. D'ARTAGNAN, the elder, ⎫
                          ⎬ D'Artagnan's parents.
MADAME D'ARTAGNAN,   ⎭

HOST OF THE JOLLY MILLER.

HOST OF THE GOLDEN LILY.

HOST OF THE GREAT ST. MARTIN TAVERN.

HOST OF THE RED DOVECOT.

LORD DE WINTER, brother-in-law of Lady de Winter.

KITTY, Lady de Winter's maid.

JACKSON, secretary of Buckingham.

LIEUTENANT JOHN FELTON, a Puritan in the service of Lord de Winter, afterwards Buckingham's assassin.

O'REILLY, a goldsmith.

CAPTAIN BUTLER, commanding an English sloop.

TWENTY YEARS AFTER.

INTRODUCTORY NOTE.

"Twenty years after" the concluding scenes of the "Three Musketeers" bring the reader to the year 1648, — the year which saw the beginning of the burlesque wars of the Fronde in France, and the grim and tragical close of the Civil War in England, with the trial and execution of Charles I., — D'Artagnan, still the typical Gascon, still lieutenant of Musketeers after twenty years of service, and somewhat inclined to repine at the ingratitude of Anne of Austria, the powerful Regent, in leaving so long unrewarded the valuable services rendered to Anne of Austria, the persecuted and despised queen, is quick to discern an opportunity to repeat the exploits of the early days.

With that object in view he sets out from Paris in search of his former companions. At Noisy he finds Aramis, who is now known as Monsieur l'Abbé d'Herblay, but whose sanctity is still largely flavored with worldliness, and whose affections have been transferred from Madame de Chevreuse to Madame la Duchesse de Longueville, sister of the "great"

Condé. She was the daughter of the beautiful Charlotte de Montmorency (*matre pulchra filia pulchrior*), and was born in the donjon at Vincennes; as she was the heart and soul of the Fronde, our hero found her lover little minded to draw his sword for Mazarin. On the confines of Picardy, on one of the estates from which he derives his high-sounding appellation of Monsieur du Vallon de Bracieux de Pierrefonds, lives Porthos, the giant, bursting with ambition to be created a baron, but still the same faithful, trusting, good-humored soul, asking but to follow wherever his cleverer friends may lead. With him D'Artagnan makes rendezvous at Paris, and departs for Blois, where he finds his former companion-in-arms, the misanthropic and melancholy, but noble-minded Athos, transformed into the Comte de la Fère. With his plebeian name he has laid aside his tendency to indulge inordinately in wine, and has become the perfect type of a French gentleman in the highest sense of the words. Dwelling on his estate of Bragelonne, near Blois, he is rearing his son (from whom the concluding work of this great series takes its name) upon his own pattern, to emulate his virtues and his accomplishments.

Our gallant friends, always one in heart and purpose, though sometimes nominally enlisted on opposite sides, count for much in the opening scenes of the extraordinary uprising against Mazarin, the Italian minister and master, if not the spouse, of the Spanish Queen-Regent, Anne of Austria. Once more, too, the reader is taken across the Channel, and made to witness, at close quarters, the final scenes in the terrible drama which was enacted on English soil.

A curious, unique episode, and impossible of occurrence in any other country than France, was the "War of the Fronde," — a war which, in the words of Voltaire, "except for the names of the King of France, the great Condé, and the capital of the kingdom, would have been as ridiculous as that of the Barberini;" a war in which no one knew why he was in arms, and in which every prominent actor changed sides so frequently that one's brain whirls with the attempt to follow the course of events; a war of couplets rather than of firearms, with women for leaders of the various factions, and cabals made and unmade by the exigencies of love affairs."

The Duchesse de Longueville shared with "La Grande Mademoiselle," the daughter of Gaston, Duc d'Orléans, the honor of being the most prominent *Frondeuse*. Mademoiselle is said to have trained the guns with her own hands upon the king's troops at the so-called "Battle of Saint-Antoine." The Duc de la Rochefoucauld, who was wounded in that affair, wrote to Madame de Longueville : —

"Pour mériter son cœur, pour plaire à ses beaux yeux,
J'ai fait la guerre aux rois ; je l'aurai faite aux dieux." *

In the memoirs of Mademoiselle appears a letter
from her father, Gaston, addressed to "Mesdames
les Comtesses, Maréchales de camp in the army of
my daughter now in the field against Mazarin."

These memoirs of Mademoiselle, with those of
Madame de Motteville, one of the queen's ladies-
in-waiting, and of the Cardinal de Retz, who figures
in these volumes as the coadjutor Archbishop of
Paris, M. de Gondy, are the principal authorities
for this period; they were the main reliance of
Voltaire in writing those portions of the "Siècle
de Louis XIV." which deal with the Fronde. There
can be no more striking testimony to the extreme
closeness with which Dumas adheres to the facts of
history in the ground-work of his romances than is
afforded by a perusal of Voltaire's chapters upon
the period covered by this narrative. Save for the
exploits of the famous four, "Twenty Years After"
might fairly be called a history of the early days
of the Fronde, so closely does the author adhere to
the historical sequence of events and their effect,
to say nothing of his accuracy in matters of detail.
The demonstration against M. Broussel and the
other councillors during the "Te Deum" for the

* To win her love, to delight her lovely eyes, I have taken
up arms against the king; I would have done the same against
the gods.

victory of Lens; the "day of the barricades;" the queen's inclination to be obstinate; the final flight to Saint-Germain, and the scarcity of bedding there; the secession of the Prince de Conti and M. de Longueville from the party of Mazarin; the battle between Condé, with eight thousand troops, and a hundred thousand bourgeois at Charenton, with the unwarlike conduct of the coadjutor's Corinth regiment, — these are by no means the only occurrences related in these pages which rest upon unquestionable authority.

The Duc de Beaufort, grandson of Henri IV. and Gabrielle d'Estrées, is one of the most picturesque figures of the period, even though his character was somewhat unstable. Not only is his escape from Vincennes described here with substantial accuracy, but the "*roi des halles,*" as he was called by the people who adored him, is himself pictured to the very life, — even to his peculiar facility in misusing words after the style of Mrs. Malaprop. It is told of him that he said one day of Madame de Grignan, who was in mourning: "I met Madame de Grignan to-day, and she looked very *lubrique*" (dissolute), — meaning to say *lugubre* (melancholy). She retaliated when she heard of it, by saying, pointing to a German nobleman who was present: "He is as like the Duc de Beaufort as one drop of water like another, except that he speaks French better than the duke." The well-known niggardliness of the thrifty Mazarin was a fair subject for M. de Beaufort's wit; and the short allowance of bed-linen on which the young king was kept by him is well authenticated.

The chapter which describes the meeting at the house of Scarron is particularly interesting for the glimpse it gives us of "the beautiful Indian," Mademoiselle François d'Aubigné. She it was who became Madame Scarron, and having been introduced into the royal circle as governess of the king's children by Madame de Montespan, at last supplanted her patroness in the affections of her august sovereign; and for thirty years ruled the kingdom of France over the shoulders of the monarch, whose unacknowledged wife she was.

It may be remarked, parenthetically, that the incident related by Athos to Madame de Chevreuse in connection with the birth of Raoul de Bragelonne is based upon an actual occurrence in the life of that somewhat eccentric lady.

Voltaire calls attention to the striking contrast, as exemplified in their widely different methods of rebelling against constituted authority, between the national characteristics of the English, " who entered into their civil troubles with melancholy implacability and fury which was carefully thought out beforehand; who took their king in battle, brought him before a court of justice, interrogated him, condemned him to death, and executed him publicly with the utmost decorum and regard for the forms of law," and those of the French, "who plunged into rebellion from mere caprice and with a smile on their lips," under the leadership of beautiful women who used their charms as a means of seducing their opponents. Witness the intrigue between Madame de Longueville and Maréchal Turenne.

This contrast has never been more strikingly brought out than in these volumes, by the gifted author who has so illumined and enlivened, with his marvellous art, many of the most entertaining and engrossing periods of French history that the history itself is made to possess tenfold interest, just as the zest of the romance is enhanced by the historical accuracy of the facts upon which it is built.

In the first of his "Roundabout Papers," Thackeray tells of a visit to Chur in the Grisons, and of a boy whom he fell in with in his walks, so absorbed in a book he was reading as to be utterly oblivious to aught else.

"What was it that so fascinated the young student as he stood by the river-shore? Not the *Pons Asinorum*. What book so delighted him, and blinded him to all the rest of the world, so that he did not care to see the apple-woman with her fruit, or (more tempting still to sons of Eve) the pretty girls with their apple cheeks, who laughed and prattled round

the fountain! What was the book? Do you suppose it was Livy, or the Greek grammar? No; it
was a NOVEL that you were reading, you lazy, not
very clean, good-for-nothing, sensible boy! It was
D'Artagnan locking up General Monk in a box, or
almost succeeding in keeping Charles the First's
head on. It was the prisoner of the Château d'If
cutting himself out of the sack fifty feet under
water (I mention the novels I like best myself —
novels without love or talking, or any of that sort
of nonsense, but containing plenty of fighting, escaping, robbery, and rescuing) — cutting himself out of
the sack, and swimming to the island of Monte
Cristo! . . . O Dumas! O thou brave, kind, gallant old Alexandre! I hereby offer thee homage
and give thee thanks for many pleasant hours. I
have read thee (being sick in bed) for thirteen hours
of a happy day, and had the ladies of the house
fighting for the volumes."

And again he says: "I think of the prodigal
banquets to which this Lucullus of a man has
invited me, with thanks and wonder. To what a
series of splendid entertainments he has treated me!
Where does he find the money for these prodigious
feasts?"

In the genial company of the author of "Esmond,"
we need not blush to enjoy the "prodigious feast"
of adventures — amusing, thrilling, and tragical —
which befall the gallant Frenchmen on both sides

of the channel. The old tie, formed twenty years before in the ranks of the musketeers, strengthened by lapse of time, by their chivalrous sympathy for fallen grandeur in the person of the ill-fated English monarch, by the shadow of the terrible scene at Armentières, and its sequel in the relentless hatred of Mordaunt, Milady's worthy son, — the old tie, we say, was too strong to be even strained by the wiles of the low-born Mazarin; so that, whether *Frondeurs* or *Cardinalists* in name, they are always true brothers-in-arms.

TWENTY YEARS AFTER.

LIST OF CHARACTERS.

Period, The Regency of Anne of Austria, 1648–1649.

ANNE OF AUSTRIA.
LOUIS XIV., at the age of ten.
HIS EMINENCE CARDINAL MAZARIN, Prime Minister of France.
BERNOUIN, his valet.
LAPORTE, attendant of the young King.
LOUIS DE BOURBON, Prince de Condé.
DUC DE CHATILLON, serving under him.
MARÉCHAL DE GRAMMONT.
COMTE DE GUICHE, his son.
M. D'ARMINGES, preceptor of Comte de Guiche.
GASTON, DUC D'ORLÉANS, the King's uncle,
DUCHESSE D'ORLÉANS,
LA GRANDE MADEMOISELLE, daughter of Gaston of Orléans.
PRINCESSE DE CONDÉ, ⎫
MARÉCHAL DE VILLEROY, ⎪
MARÉCHAL DE MEILLERAIE, ⎪
FONTRAILLES, his aide-de-camp. ⎬ of the Court.
M. DE FLAMARENS, ⎪
CHANCELLOR SÉGUIER, ⎪
ABBÉ DE LA RIVIÈRE, ⎪
CHEVALIER DE COISLIN, ⎭
MADAME DE MOTTEVILLE, ⎫
SOCRATIN, her sister, ⎪
MADAME DE BRÉGY, ⎬ the Queen's ladies.
MADEMOISELLE DE BEAUMONT, ⎪
MADAME BEAUVAIS, ⎭

BÉRINGHEN, the Queen's first valet de chambre.

M. D'ÉMERY, Superintendent of Finances.

M. BLANCMESNIL, President of the Parliament.

M. DU TREMBLAY, Governor of the Bastille.

M. DE CHAVIGNY, Governor of Vincennes Prison.

LA RAMÉE,   } officers at Vincennes.
M. DE POINS,

M. D'ARTAGNAN, lieutenant in the King's Musketeers.

M. DE BELLIÈRE,
M. DU VERGER,   } Musketeers.
M. DE CAMBON,
M. DE LILLEBONNE,

M. DE GUITAUT, captain of the Queen's Guards.

M. DE COMMINGES, lieutenant of the Queen's Guards.

M. DE SAINT-LAURENT, of the Queen's Guards.

M. DE VILLEQUIER, captain of the King's Guards.

NOGENT BEAUTIN, the Court Fool.

COMTE DE LA FÈRE (formerly called Athos).

VICOMTE DE BRAGELONNE, his son.

CHEVALIER D'HERBLAY (Aramis).

M. DU VALLON DE BRACIEUX DE PIERREFONDS (Porthos).

MOUSQUETON, his servant.

MADEMOISELLE LOUISE DE LA VALLIÈRE.

MADAME DE SAINT-REMY, her mother.

ABBÉ SCARRON.

CHAUPERROIS, his servant.

MADEMOISELLE FRANÇOISE D'AUBIGNÉ, afterwards Madame
Scarron and Madame de Maintenon.

MADEMOISELLE PAULET

M. MENAGE.

M. DE SCUDÉRY.

MADEMOISELLE DE SCUDÉRY.

LA BRUYÈRE,   } soldiers on guard at Rueil.
BARTHOIS,

THE CURATE OF BÉTHUNE.

THE EXECUTIONER OF BÉTHUNE.

DAME NANETTE, servant of Councillor Broussel.

M. PÉREZ, landlord of Bedford's tavern.

FRONDEURS.

DUC DE BEAUFORT, grandson of Henri IV.

DUCHESSE DE LONGUEVILLE.

DUCHESSE DE CHEVREUSE.

DUC DE LONGUEVILLE.

DUC DE CHEVREUSE.

PRINCE DE CONTI.

DUC D'ELBŒUF.

DUC DE BOUILLON.

MARECHAL DE LA MOTHE.

M. DE LUYNES.

MARQUIS DE VITRY.

PRINCE DE MARCILLAC.

MARQUIS DE NOIRMOUTIERS.

COMTE DE FIESQUE.

MARQUIS DE LAIGUES.

COMTE DE MONTRÉSOR.

MARQUIS DE SÉVIGNÉ.

M. DE BRISSAC.

M. DE CHANLEU.

ABBÉ JEAN FRANÇOIS DE GONDY, the Coadjutor, afterwards
Cardinal de Retz.

COMTE DE ROCHEFORT.

COUNCILLOR BROUSSEL.

LOUVIÈRES, his son.

CHEVALIER D'HUMIÈRES.

PLANCHET, formerly D'Artagnan's servant, now a confectioner.

BAZIN, beadle at Notre Dame.

PRIESTS OF ST. MERRI, ST. SULPICE, AND ST. EUSTACHE.

MAILLARD, a mendicant.

MADELAINE TURQUAINE, hostess of the Hôtel de la Chevrette, D'Artagnan's lodgings.

FRIQUET, a choir-boy at Notre Dame.

GRIMAUD,
CHARLOT,
OLIVAIN, } servants of Comte de la Fère.
BLASOIS,

BOISJOLI, servant of Duc de Beaufort.

NOIRMONT, the Duc de Beaufort's steward.

HOST OF THE CYGNE DE LA CROIX.

GROS LOUIS, a farmer at St. Germain.

LANDLORD OF THE CROWNED SHEEP.

URBAIN, a soldier attending on Comte de Guiche.

ENGLISH.

CHARLES I., King of England.

HENRIETTA OF FRANCE, his wife.

THE PRINCESS HENRIETTA,
THE PRINCESS CHARLOTTE, } his children.
THE DUKE OF GLOUCESTER,

OLIVER CROMWELL.

COLONEL HARRISON,
CAPTAIN GROSLOW, } officers in Cromwell's army.
COLONEL TOMLINSON,

PRESIDENT BRADSHAW, of the High Court, trying Charles I.

LADY FAIRFAX.

BISHOP JUXON.

JOHN FRANCIS DE WINTER, in the service of Cromwell, under the name of Mordaunt.

LORD DE WINTER, his uncle.

PARRY, servant of Charles I.

EARL OF LEVEN.

PATRICK, a sailor.

VICOMTE DE BRAGELONNE.

INTRODUCTORY NOTE.

THE "Vicomte de Bragelonne," the longest and in
many respects the most powerful of the D'Artagnan
series, was first presented to the English-speaking
public in an unabridged translation, conforming to
the author's own arrangement and in readable form,
by the present publishers. Owing to its great
length it had previously been translated only in
an abridged form. Detached portions of it, too,
have appeared from time to time. The chapters
devoted to Mademoiselle de la Vallière have been
published separately under the title of "Louise de
la Vallière," while what is commonly known as
"The Iron Mask" is a translation of that portion
of Bragelonne which relates the attempted substi-
tution of the Bastille prisoner for Louis XIV.

The romance, as it was written and as it is here
presented in English, offers a marvellously faithful
picture of the French court from a period immediately preceding the young king's marriage to his
cousin, Maria Theresa, the Infante of Spain, to the

downfall of Fouquet. This period was a momentous one for France, embracing as it did the diplomatic triumph of Mazarin in the advantageous
Treaty of the Pyrenees; the death of that avaricious
and unscrupulous, but eminently able and far-seeing,
minister and cardinal; the assumption of power by
Louis in person; and the rise to high office and
influence over the crushed and disgraced Fouquet,
of Jean-Baptiste Colbert. These two years marked
the beginning of the most brilliant epoch of court
life in France, as well as of her greatest, if somewhat factitious, glory both at home and abroad.

The historical accuracy of the author of "Bragelonne" — which Miss Pardoe, in her justly popular
and entertaining work on Louis XIV., and the
historian Michelet as well, have so strongly maintained — is perhaps more striking in this than in
any other of his romances. It is not only in the
matter of the events of greater or less importance
that one familiar with the history of the period seems
to be reading some contemporary chronicle, but the
character-sketches of the prominent personages are
drawn with such entire fidelity to life that we seem
to see the very men and women themselves as they
appeared to their contemporaries.

Thus it is with the king, whose intense egotism
was beginning to develop, being unceasingly fos-
tered by the flattery of those who surrounded him
and told him that he was the greatest of men and

kings, invincible in arms and unequalled in wisdom; who was rapidly reaching that state of sublime self-sufficiency which led to the famous saying: "L'État, c'est moi;" but who was, nevertheless, more bashful and timid and humble at the feet of the gentle and retiring La Vallière than if she had been the greatest queen in Christendom.

Of his favorites La Vallière was the only one who loved him for himself alone, and she has come down to us as one of the few Frenchwomen who have ever been ashamed of being known as a king's mistress. Her life is faithfully sketched in these pages, from her first glimpse of the king at Blois, when she gave her heart to him unasked. When the scheme was formed to use her as a cloak for the king's flirtation with Madame Henriette, "there was a rumor connecting her name with that of a certain Vicomte de Bragelonne, who had caused her young heart to utter its first sighs in Blois; but the most malicious gossips spoke of it only as a childish flame, — that is to say, utterly without importance."

Mademoiselle de Montalais made herself notorious as a go-between in various love affairs, while Mademoiselle de Tonnay-Charente, otherwise Mademoiselle de Rochechouart-Mortemart, clever and beautiful, was destined, as Madame de Montespan, to supplant her modest friend in the affections of their lord and master; and after a career of unexampled brilliancy to be herself supplanted by the governess of her legitimated children, the widow Scarron, better known as Madame la Marquise de Maintenon.

"Une maîtresse tonnante et triomphante," Madame de Sévigné calls Madame de Montespan. The Mortemart family was supposed to be of the greatest antiquity and to have the same origin as the English Mortimers. The *esprit de Mortemart*, or Mortemart wit, was reputed to be an inalienable characteristic of the race. And what of Madame herself, who played a part at the court of France which was almost exactly duplicated forty years later by her granddaughter, the Savoy princess, who became Duchesse de Bourgogne, and whose untimely death was one of the most severe of the many domestic afflictions which darkened the last years of the old king's life? Let us listen for a moment to Robert Louis Stevenson, writing of the "Vicomte de Bragelonne" after his fifth or sixth perusal of it: —

"Madame enchants me. I can forgive that royal minx her most serious offences; I can thrill and soften with the king on that memorable occasion when he goes to upbraid and remains to flirt; and when it comes to the 'Allons, aimez-moi donc,' it is my heart that melts in the bosom of De Guiche."

The mutual passion of De Guiche and Madame lasted all her life, we are told; and yet, alas! it was but short-lived, for Madame's days were numbered. She died in 1670, after an illness of but a few hours, regretted by everybody except her husband. There is little doubt that she was poisoned through the instrumentality of the Chevalier de Lorraine, and probably with the connivance of Monsieur, whose favorite he was. The Chevalier was a prodigy of vice, and one of the most unsavory characters of the period.

The greed and avarice of Mazarin were his most prominent characteristics; they are illustrated by innumerable anecdotes, one of which may perhaps be repeated here: He had been informed that a pamphlet was about to be put on sale, in which he was shamefully libelled; he confiscated it, and of course the market price of it at once increased enormously; whereupon he sold it secretly at an exorbitant figure and allowed it to circulate, pocketing a thousand pistoles as his share of the transaction. He used to tell of this himself, and laugh heartily over it. His supreme power had endured so long that everybody desired his death, and his contemporaries hardly did justice to the very solid benefits he had procured for France.

In drawing the characters of Fouquet and Colbert, Dumas has perhaps, as Mr. Stevenson says, shown an inclination to enlist his reader's sympathies for the former against his own judgment of the equities of the case.

"Historic justice," says the essayist, "should be all upon the side of Colbert, of official honesty and fiscal competence. And Dumas knows it well; three times at least he shows his knowledge, — once it is but flashed upon us and received with the laughter of Fouquet himself, in the jesting controversy in the gardens of Saint-Mandé; once it is touched on by Aramis in the forest of Sénart; in the end it is set before us clearly in one dignified speech of the triumphant Colbert. But in Fouquet — the master, the lover of good cheer and wit and art, the swift transactor of much business, *l'homme de bruit, l'homme de plaisir, l'homme qui n'est que parceque les autres sont* — Dumas saw something of himself, and drew the figure the more tenderly; it is to me even touching to see how he insists on Fouquet's honor."

The grand fête at Vaux was the last straw which made the superintendent's downfall absolutely certain. "If his disgrace had not already been determined upon in the king's mind, it would have been at Vaux. . . . As there was but one sun in heaven, there could be but one king in France."

It is interesting to read that the execution of the order for Fouquet's arrest was entrusted to one *D'Artagnan*, Captain of Musketeers, "a man of action, entirely unconnected with all the cabals, and who, during his thirty-three years' experience in the Musketeers, had never known anything outside of his orders."

Fouquet lived nearly twenty years in prison,

and died in 1680. He has been connected in various ways with the "Man with the Iron Mask," some investigators having maintained that he was identical with that individual, and therefore could not have died in 1680; while others have claimed that the Iron Mask was imprisoned at the Château of Pignerol while Fouquet was there. The legend of the unfortunate prisoner has given rise to much investigation and to many conjectures. Voltaire bent his energies to solve the mystery, and in our own day M. Marius Topin has gone into the subject most exhaustively, but without reaching a satisfactory conclusion as to the identity of the sufferer. The somewhat audacious use made of the legend by Dumas is based upon what was at one time a favorite solution; namely, that the unknown was a brother of Louis XIV., said by some to have been a twin, and by others to have been some years older and of doubtful paternity.

It would be an endless task to cite all the portions of these volumes in which historical facts are related with substantial accuracy; in them fact and fiction are so blended that each enhances the charm of the other, — the element of authenticity adding zest and interest to the romantic portions, while the element of romance gives life and color to the narration of facts.

Our old friends of the earlier tales bear us company nearly to the end; but for the first time,

political interests are allowed to interfere with the
perfect confidence that has existed between them:
Aramis, as General of the Jesuits, is true to the
reputation of the order, and hesitates at no dis-
simulation to gain his ambitious ends. Porthos,
still blindly faithful to that one of his friends who
claims his allegiance, falls at last a victim to his
childlike trust in the scheming prelate, and dies
the death of a veritable Titan. The magnificent
outburst of righteous anger which the Comte de la
Fère visits upon the king is the last expiring gleam
of the spirit of the Athos of the Musketeers.
Wrapped up in his love for the heart-broken Bragelonne, he lives only in his life and "dies in his
death."

And D'Artagnan? His praises and his requiem
have been most fittingly and lovingly sounded by
the same graceful writer who has already been
quoted, and in the same essay, entitled "Gossip
upon a Novel of Dumas," —

"It is in the character of D'Artagnan that we must
look for that spirit of morality which is one of the
chief merits of the book, makes one of the main joys
of its perusal, and sets it high above more popular
rivals. . . . He has mellowed into a man so witty,
rough, kind, and upright that he takes the heart by
storm. There is nothing of the copy-book about his
virtues, nothing of the drawing-room in his fine natural
civility ; he will sail near the wind ; he is no district

visitor, no Wesley or Robespierre; his conscience is void of all refinement, whether for good or evil; but the whole man rings true like a good sovereign. . . . Here and throughout, if I am to choose virtues for myself or my friends, let me choose the virtues of D'Artagnan. I do not say that there is no character as well drawn in Shakespeare; I do say there is none that I love so wholly. . . . No part of the world has ever seemed to me so charming as these pages; and not even my friends are quite so real, perhaps quite so dear, as D'Artagnan."

Of the great closing chapters of the book, in which the friends are at last separated by death, D'Artagnan falling on the battle-field just as he was about to grasp the coveted prize of the baton of a marshal of France, Stevenson says : —

"I can recall no other work of the imagination in which the end of life is represented with so nice a tact; . . . and above all, in the last volume, I find a singular charm of spirit. It breathes a pleasant and a tonic sadness, always brave, never hysterical. Upon the crowded, noisy life of this long tale, evening gradually falls, and the lights are extinguished, and the heroes pass away one by one. One by one they go, and not a regret embitters their departure. The young succeed them in their places. Louis Quatorze is swelling larger and shining broader; another generation and another France dawn on the horizon, — but for us and these old men whom we have loved so long, the inevitable end draws near and is welcome. To read this well is to anticipate experience. Ah! if only when these hours of the long shadows fall for us in reality and not in figure, we may hope to face them with a mind as quiet. But my paper is running out; the siege-guns are firing on the Dutch frontier, and I must say adieu for the fifth time to my old comrade, fallen on the field of glory. Adieu, rather *au revoir!* Yet a sixth time, dearest D'Artagnan, we shall kidnap Monk and take horse together for Belle Isle."

VICOMTE DE BRAGELONNE.

LIST OF CHARACTERS.

Period, 1660–1671.

Louis XIV., King of France.
Maria Theresa, his Queen.
Anne of Austria, the Queen Mother.
Gaston of Orléans, uncle of the King.
Duchesse d'Orléans,
Philippe, Duc d'Anjou, brother of the King, afterwards Duc d'Orléans.
Henrietta of England, his wife.
Cardinal Mazarin.
Bernouin, his valet.
Brienne, his secretary.
M. le Duc de Beaufort.
Prince de Condé.
Chevalier de Lorraine, favorite of Philippe d'Orléans.
Comte de Saint-Aignan, attending on the King.
Mademoiselle Marie de Mancini, niece of Cardinal Mazarin.
Mademoiselle Aure de Montalais,
Mlle. Athenaise de Tonnay-Charente, afterwards Madame de Montespan,
Mademoiselle Louise de la Vallière,
} Maids of Honor to Henrietta, Duchesse d'Orléans.
La Molina, Anne of Austria's Spanish nurse.
Duchesse de Chevreuse.
Madame de Motteville,
Madame de Navailles,
Mademoiselle de Châtillon,
Comtesse de Soissons,
Mademoiselle Arnoux,
} ladies of the French Court.

LOUISE DE KÉROUALLE, afterwards Duchess of Portsmouth.
MARÉCHAL GRAMMONT.
COMTE DE GUICHE, his son, in love with Madame Henrietta.
M. DE MANICAMP, friend of the Comte de Guiche.
M. DE MALICORNE, in love with Mademoiselle de Montalais.
M. D'ARTAGNAN, Lieutenant, afterwards Captain, of the King's
　　Musketeers.
COMTE DE LA FÈRE (Athos).
RAOUL, VICOMTE DE BRAGELONNE, his son.
M. D'HERBLAY, afterwards Bishop of Vannes, General of the
　　Order of Jesuits, and Duc d'Alaméda (Aramis).
BARON DU VALLON DE BRACIEUX DE PIERREFONDS (Porthos)
JEAN POQUELIN DE MOLIÈRE.
VICOMTE DE WARDES.
M. DE VILLEROY.
M. DE FOUQUET, Superintendent of Finance.
MADAME FOUQUET, his wife.
MESSIEURS LYONNE AND LETELLIER, Fouquet's associates in
　　the ministry.
MARQUISE DE BELLIÈRE, in love with Fouquet.
M. DE LA FONTAINE, ⎫
M. GOURVILLE, 　　　 ⎪
M. PELLISSON, 　　　 ⎬ friends of Fouquet.
M. CONRART, 　　　　⎪
M. LORET, 　　　　　⎭
L'ABBÉ FOUQUET, brother of the Superintendent.
M. VANEL, a Councillor of Parliament, afterwards Procureur-
　　Général.
MARGUERITE VANEL, his wife, a rival of la Marquise de la Bellière.
M. DE SAINT-REMY, maître-hotel to Gaston of Orléans.
MADAME DE SAINT-REMY.
JEAN-BAPTISTE COLBERT, Intendant of Finance, afterwards Prime
　　Minister.
MESSIEURS D'INFREVILLE, DESTOUCHES, AND FORANT, in Col-
　　bert's service.

MESSIEURS BRETEUIL, MARIN, AND HAVARD, colleagues of Colbert.

MESSIEURS D'EYMERIS, LYODOT, AND VANIN, Farmers-General

M. DE BAISEMAUX DE MONTLEZUN, Governor of the Bastille.

SELDON, a prisoner at the Bastille.

No. 3, BERTAUDIÈRE, afterwards "The Iron Mask."

M. DE SAINT-MARS, Governor of Ile Sainte Marguerite.

A FRANCISCAN FRIAR, General of the Order of Jesuits.

BARON VON WOSTPUR,

MONSEIGNEUR HERREBIA,

MEINHEER BONSTETT,

SIGNOR MARINI, } Jesuits.

LORD MACCUMNOR,

GRISART, a physician.

LOUIS CONSTANT DE PRESSIGNY, Captain of the King's Frigate "Pomona."

M. DE GESVRES, Captain of the King's Guards.

M. DE BISCARRAT, an officer of the King's Guards.

M. DE FRIEDRICH, an officer of the Swiss Guards.

MESSIRE JEAN PERCERIN, the King's tailor.

M. VALOT, the King's physician.

PLANCHET, a confectioner in the Rue des Lombards.

MADAME GECHTER, his housekeeper.

DADDY CÉLESTIN, Planchet's servant.

BAZIN, servant to M. d'Herblay.

GRIMAUD, an old servant of Athos.

MOUSQUETON, servant of Porthos.

BLASOIS, servant to Athos.

OLIVAIN, servant of Vicomte de Bragelonne.

JUPENET, a printer,

GÉTARD, an architect, } in the service of Fouquet.

DANICAMP,

MENNEVILLE, an adventurer.

M. LEBRUN, painter.

M. FAUCHEUX, a goldsmith.

VATEL, Fouquet's steward.

TOBY, one of Fouquet's servants.

YVES, a sailor.

KEYSER, a Dutch fisherman.

MAÎTRE CROPOLE, of the hostelry of the Medici at Blois.

PITTRINO, his assistant.

MADAME CROPOLE.

LANDLORD OF THE BEAU PAON HOTEL.

SUPERIOR OF THE CARMELITE CONVENT AT CHAILLOT.

GUÉNAUD, Mazarin's physician.

THE THÉATIN FATHER, The Cardinal's spiritual director.

ENGLISH.

CHARLES II., King of England.

PARRY, his servant.

GENERAL MONK, afterwards Duke of Albemarle.

DIGBY, his aide-de-camp.

GENERAL LAMBERT.

JAMES, Duke of York, brother of Charles II.

GEORGE VILLIERS, Duke of Buckingham.

LORD ROCHESTER.

DUKE OF NORFOLK.

MISS MARY GRAFTON.

MISS STEWART.

HOST OF THE STAG'S HORN TAVERN.

THE BLACK TULIP.

INTRODUCTORY NOTE.

THE 20th of August, 1672, was by no means the first occasion on which the Dutch had demonstrated their claim to the very highest rank among ungrateful peoples.

Witness the pathetic figure of the " Great Deliverer," the first William of Orange, fighting almost single-handed the whole mighty power of Philip II., and standing alone amid the jealous envy of those whose release from a hateful, galling despotism was his only purpose in life. He founded the Dutch Republic *in spite of* his fellow-countrymen, rather than in concert with them; and it was not until the hand of the paid assassin struck him down that they knew how truly he had been the " Father William " of them and their country.

Who that has read in Motley's engrossing pages the story of John of Olden-Barneveldt has not been lost in wonder (and in disgust) at the blind, unreasoning spirit of jealousy and distrust, which persistently thwarted the earnest, devoted, single-hearted efforts of that great-souled man, which accused him, of all men on earth, of treachery and subserviency to the enemies of the Republic, and which finally inflicted upon him the most shameful of all deaths, — death upon the gallows ?

The fate of Olden-Barneveldt emphasizes, more strongly than any other single circumstance, that characteristic of the Dutch, which has always made it impossible for them to reap the full benefit of the lessons which they have taught to other nations by their persistent, self-sacrificing heroism.

The later exemplification of the same character-istic in the scene described in the opening chapters of "The Black Tulip" was only the less striking in so far as the services of the De Witts to the Republic had been less eminent and noteworthy than those of Barneveldt, whose lot it was to live at a more momentous epoch.

As in the earlier period the great Pensionary fell a victim to the machinations of Prince Maurice of Orange, or of those who used his revered name as a cloak for their designs, while they scattered broadcast the charge that Barneveldt was engaged in secret and traitorous negotiations with Spain, that is to say, with the power, against which his whole life was one long tireless struggle: so were the De Witts sacrificed to the youthful ambition of another Prince of Orange, who allowed himself to be made the tool of the envious detractors of the patriotic brothers, so far as to give at least his silent assent to the pitiless persecution which ended so fatally. The subsequent career of this prince upon the English throne did much to efface this blot upon his fame.

The passionate fondness of this same people for the peaceful art of floriculture and the historical Harlem tulip craze furnished M. Dumas with a congenial theme, which, interwoven with the incident of the deposit with the innocent tulip-fancier of the Grand Pensionary's correspondence with the awe-inspiring Court of France, was worked over by the matchless story-teller into the romance of "The Black Tulip."

THE BLACK TULIP.

LIST OF CHARACTERS.

Period, 1672-1675.

WILLIAM, PRINCE OF ORANGE, afterward William III. King of England.

LOUIS XIV., King of France.

CORNELIUS DE WITT, inspector of dikes at the Hague.

JOHN DE WITT, his brother, Grand Pensionary of Holland.

COLONEL VAN DEKEN, aide-de-camp to William of Orange.

DR. CORNELIUS VAN BAERLE, a tulip-fancier, godson of Cornelius de Witt.

MYNHEER ISAAC BOXTEL, his rival.

MARQUIS DE LOUVOIS.

COUNT TILLY, Captain of the Cavalry of the Hague.

MYNHEER BOWELT, } deputies.
MYNHEER D'ASPEREN, }

THE RECORDER OF THE STATES.

MASTER VAN SPENSER, a magistrate at Dort.

TYCKALAER, a surgeon at the Hague.

GERARD DOW.

MYNHEER VAN SYSTENS, Burgomaster of Harlem and President of its Horticultural Society.

CRAEKE, confidential servant of John de Witt.

GRYPHUS, a jailer.

ROSA, his daughter, in love with Cornelius van Baerle.

CHEVALIER D'HARMENTAL.

INTRODUCTORY NOTE.

THE eight years from the death of Louis XIV., in
1715, to the legal majority of his great-grandson
and successor, Louis XV., in 1723, exhibited a state
of affairs in France corresponding very closely with
that which existed in England after the Restoration
of 1660, — when the natural reaction from the
supremacy of the pleasure-hating, psalm-singing
saints of the Commonwealth carried the nation
to hitherto unheard-of excesses in the opposite
direction.

During the last thirty years of the reign of the
"Grand Monarque," piety had come to be the
fashion at the French Court, of which Madame de
Maintenon, the king's unacknowledged wife, was
the true, though uncrowned, queen.

"Louis XIV., in his old age, became religious,"
says Macaulay in one of his critical essays; "he
determined that his subjects should be religious,
too; he shrugged his shoulders and knitted his
brows if he observed at his levee or near his

dinner-table any gentleman who neglected the duties enjoined by the Church, and rewarded piety with blue ribbons, invitations to Marly, governments, pensions, and regiments. Forthwith Versailles became, in everything but dress, a convent. The pulpits and confessionals were surrounded by swords and embroidery. The Marshals of France were much in prayer; and there was hardly one among the dukes and peers who did not carry good little books in his pocket, fast during Lent, and communicate at Easter. Madame de Maintenon, who had a great share in the blessed work, boasted that devotion had become quite the fashion."

But Louis XIV. died. His will was treated with scant ceremony by the Parliament of Paris; his legitimized sons were pulled down from the height to which he, with the cordial approval of their former governess, Madame de Maintenon, had elevated them; and Philippe, Duc d'Orléans, whose private morals were the very antithesis of all that had been held in high esteem at court for a generation, was placed at the head of the government during the minority of the young king.

The many excellent qualities of the regent were overshadowed, in his own day as they have been for posterity, by the shameless profligacy of his life.

When the royal power, substantially unlimited, was placed in his hands, the whole face of the court changed; and unblushing debauchery succeeded to the odor of sanctity which had so long filled the nostrils of the courtiers. Madame de Maintenon was discredited; Père le Tellier, the bigoted confessor of the late king, vanished from the public gaze; while those whose real or pretended piety had led them to espouse the cause of the Duc du Maine as against the regent, had nothing to hope for under the new administration. Add to this that the father, mother, and brother of the child who had become king had all died within a week of one another some three years before; that his own life had been saved at the same time only by a miracle, and that very many people, under the guidance of a few who pretended to believe it, honestly did believe that the Duc d'Orléans was responsible for all these casualties; while the throne of Spain was filled by a grandson of Louis XIV., himself a candidate for the regency, bitterly jealous of the regent, and an inevitable candidate for the throne in case of the death of the sickly child, whose life was supposed to be in hourly danger. To be sure, by the terms of the Treaty of Utrecht, Philippe V. solemnly renounced all claim to the throne of France; but the emptiness of such renunciations had been abundantly demonstrated in the case of his great-grandmother, Anne of Austria, wife of Louis XIII., and his grandmother, Marie Thérèse, wife of Louis XIV.; and even Saint-Simon, the most devoted of all the friends of the regent, tells us in his Memoirs that if Louis XV. had died he should have been obliged, tearfully and with great regret, to espouse the cause of the representative of the elder line. Under these circumstances, some sort of a plot against the government of the regent was inevitable. The so-called "Conspiracy of Cellamare," formed to carry out a far-reaching scheme of the ambitious and restless intriguer, Cardinal Alberoni, the all-powerful minister of Philippe V., forms the ground-work upon which Dumas has built the "Chevalier d'Harmental."

That the epithet "far-reaching" is not misapplied to the scheme of the ex-bell-ringer of Parma, will be apparent upon perusal of the objects he had in view, which are set forth with fulness and accuracy in the following pages ; but the *dénouement* contained many elements of burlesque. Indeed, despite the undoubted earnestness of the Duchesse du Maine and the poisoned pen of the atrabilious poet, La Grange Chancel, the "Court" of Sceaux, with its "Order of the Honey-Bee," was a burlesque in itself, and the conspirators at the French end were mere playthings in the hands of the clever and unscrupulous Dubois. It is a curious fact that the Duchess, who was a legitimate princess of the blood (she and her sister were called "dolls of the blood" in allusion to their diminutive size), was the life and soul of a plot to elevate the late king's illegitimate progeny over the heads of the legitimate princes, while her husband, the principal beneficiary of the plot, was very lukewarm in forwarding it. and had to be continually urged on by her. It is said that while Louis XIV. was at the point of death, the Duc du Maine persisted in neglecting his own interests to devote himself to a translation of Lucretius, so that his wife said to him contemptuously: "You will wake some fine morning to find yourself a member of the Academy, and the Duc d'Orléans Regent of France."

For the character of the Duc du Maine it is hard to feel any emotion but contempt; while it is equally hard to avoid feeling something like sympathy for the perpetual disappointments of his restless, intriguing little wife. Her character is best studied in the extremely entertaining memoirs of Mademoiselle de Launay, better known as Madame de Staal, but who must not be confounded with the more celebrated Madame de Staël (born Mademoiselle Necker) of the Revolutionary era.

There is, indeed, no other source from which so much information as to the inside workings of the "Conspiracy of Cellamare" can be obtained. "Little" de Launay was an extremely clever young woman, and when the bubble burst, she abundantly justified the confidence the conspirators had placed in her discretion. It is evident from her own naïve disclosures that the old Abbé Chaulieu was not the only one of the "Knights of the Honey-Bee" who offered love to her; but he was so old that his ardent passion was a fair theme of gossip and pleasantry. "The abbé often proposed to make me handsome presents," she says, "in addition to the incense he poured out at my feet. Being somewhat annoyed one day by his persistence in urging me to accept a thousand pistoles, I said to him: 'As a mark of my gratitude for your generous offers I give you this advice: don't make similar ones to many women or you may find one who will take you at your word.' 'Oh!' said he, 'I know whom I am dealing with.' This naïve response made me laugh."

The finishing touch was put, to the exasperation of Madame du Maine, by the outcome of the famous Bed of Justice of August, 1718, which is referred to by Dumas. Her appeals to Alberoni for a speedy beginning of operations became frantic; and the

negotiations through Cellamare were rapidly drawing to a point, when Dubois thought fit to show his
hand, and the farce was at an end.   That the
brewing of the conspiracy had long been known to
Dubois admits of little doubt; the circumstances
which immediately led to the pricking of the
bubble have been variously related.

Voltaire (Précis du Siècle de Louis XV.) gives
the credit of putting Dubois upon the scent to La
Fillon, "a courtesan who had risen from the lowest
slums to become a celebrated procuress.   She had
long been in the pay of Dubois, who had recently
become Secretary for Foreign Affairs."   As told by
Voltaire, the responsibility for the premature disclosure rests with the Abbé de Porto-Carrero, an
attaché of the Spanish Embassy and an habitué
of the establishment of La Fillon, where certain
papers were filched from him as he was on the
point of setting out for Spain.   The papers were
handed over to Dubois, by whose orders Porto-
Carrero was pursued and overtaken at Poitiers.
All his papers were seized, with the result described by Dumas.   The Fillon incident is rejected
by M. Henri Martin, but is accepted by Michelet;
it is mentioned in all the contemporary memoirs,
too; and as Voltaire was in Paris at the time, there
seems to be good reason to believe that it rests

upon a foundation of fact. There is also excellent authority for the Buvat incident, substantially as here related. Jean Buvat was a clerk at the Bibliothèque, who eked out his very slender pay by copying. He was the author of certain memoirs which exist only in manuscript, but are deemed of much value by historical writers, especially as to the exciting scenes incident to the rise and progress of the "Mississippi" scheme and the financial "system" of John Law.

The customary accuracy of the gifted author, both in the delineation of character and the relation of incident, is to be noted in the "Chevalier d'Harmental." With the exception of the hero himself and Bathilde, and the scenes which deal with their mutual attachment, hardly a person is mentioned who was not a prominent figure of the time; hardly an event, however trivial, is referred to which did not actually happen.

In Madame de Staal-de Launay's entertaining pages, we meet Malezieux, Brigaud, Pompadour, Baron de Valef (Walef), the Comte de Laval, and "le beau Cardinal de Polignac," who continued to conspire for many years afterward whenever he saw a chance.

During the first three quarters of the eighteenth century, there was no time when Richelieu, the fribble, failed to occupy a prominence which was as absurd as it was humiliating to the court which permitted it. While he was confined in the Bastille (for the third time) for his idiotic share in the Cellamare affair, he was visited by two royal princesses, disguised as laundresses, — Mademoiselle de Charolais, a descendant of the great Condé, and Mademoiselle de Valois, the regent's daughter. The latter was finally married to the Duke of Modena to remove her from the sphere of Richelieu's influence. It is said that she voluntarily exposed herself to infection from the small-pox to escape the distasteful match; but she was at last compelled to leave France. She gave vent to her sentiments in the following punning verses: —

"J'épouse un des plus petits princes,
Maître des très-petits états,
Quatre desquels ne vaudraient pas
Une de nos moindres provinces.
Nul jeu: finance très-petite:
Quelle différence, grand Dieu!
Entre ce triste et *pauvre lieu*,
Et le *riche lieu* que je quitte!"

It should perhaps be noticed that the author has somewhat ante-dated the elevation of Dubois to the archbishopric of Cambrai, which did not actually take place until 1720. The necessary preliminaries to his elevation, arising from the facts that he was not in holy orders and was a married man, were accomplished as described. The Comte de Nocé, who stood closest to the regent of all the *roués*, said to him, apropos of this appointment: "What! That man Archbishop of Cambrai! Why, you told me yourself that he was a miserable, worthless, unbelieving dog."

"So he is," said the regent, "and that's just the reason why I have made the appointment; when he's an archbishop he will have to go to communion."

While there is much in the character of the Duc d'Orléans which merits the severest condemnation and little to command actual respect, his vices were after all those of a deplorably weak rather than a wicked man. It can fairly be said that he never purposely injured a human being; and history furnishes ample justification for relieving the gloomy picture of his slavish subserviency to his own passions and to·the will of his crafty minister and ex-preceptor, by ascribing to him such generous deeds as that with which this story closes.

LE

CHEVALIER D'HARMENTAL.

LIST OF CHARACTERS.

Period, 1718.

Louis XV., at the age of nine.
Philippe, Duc d'Orléans, his uncle, the Regent of France.
Duchesse d'Orléans, his wife.
Madame Elizabeth Charlotte, Princess Palatine, the
  Regent's mother.
Duchesse de Berri,
Louise-Adelaide d'Orléans,
Mademoiselle de Chartres, } the Regent's
Mademoiselle Aglaé de Valois, } daughters.
Princess Louise, afterward Queen of Spain,
Mademoiselle Elizabeth, afterward Duch-
  esse de Lorraine,
Abbé Dubois, the Regent's Minister of State.
André Hercule de Fleury, Archbishop of Fréjus, preceptor
  to the young King.
Madame de Maintenon.
Duke of Berwick, Lieutenant-General of the French armies.
Adrien Maurice, Duc de Noailles, President of the Council
  of Finance.
Maréchal d'Uxelles, President of the Council of Foreign
  Affairs.
Duc d'Antin, Superintendent of Ships.
Bishop of Troyes.
Bishop of Nantes.
M. de Launay, Governor of the Bastille.

PRINCE DE CONDÉ,
LOUIS HENRI, DUC DE BOURBON,
DUC DE SAINT-SIMON,
LOUIS ALEXANDRE DE BOURBON,
    COMTE DE TOULOUSE,
DUC DE LAFORCE,
CHEVALIER DE RAVANNE,
MARQUIS DE LAVRILLIÈRE,
MARQUIS D'EFFIAT,
MARQUIS DE TORCY,
MARÉCHAL DE VILLARS,
MARÉCHAL D'ESTRÉES,   gentlemen of the French
MARÉCHAL DE BEZONS,   Court.
MARQUIS DE CANILLAC,
CHEVALIER DE SIMIANE,
COMTE DE FARGY,
DUC DE GUICHE,
COMTE DE NOCÉ,
DUC DE BRANCAS,
MARQUIS DE BROGLIE,
MARQUIS DE PARABÈRE,
COMTE DE GACÉ,
M. LEBLANC,
MESSIRE VOYER D'ARGENSON, Lieutenant of Police.
MARQUIS DE LAFARE, Captain of the Guards.
MONSIEUR D'ARTAGNAN, Captain of the Gray Musketeers.
MARQUIS DE SABRAN, maître-d'-hôtel to the Regent.
MARQUISE DE PARABÈRE,
DUCHESSE DE FALARIS,
MADAME SOPHIE D'AVERNE,
MARQUISE DE SABRAN,   ladies of the French Court.
MADEMOISELLE SALERI,
MADAME DE TENCIN,
MADEMOISELLE DE CHAROLAIS,
MADAME DE MOUCHY, lady of honor to Duchesse de Berri.
MADAME DE PONS, tire-woman to Duchesse de Berri.

PHILIP V. of Spain,
CARDINAL ALBERONI,
MONSIEUR LE DUC DU MAINE, son of Louis
    XIV. and Madame de Montespan,
LOUISE BÉNÉDICTE DE CONDÉ, Duchesse du
    Maine,
CARDINAL MELCHIOR DE POLIGNAC,
LOUIS FRANÇOIS ARMAND DU PLESSIS, DUC
    DE RICHELIEU,
MARQUIS DE POMPADOUR,
MONSIEUR DE MALEZIEU, Chancellor of
    Dombes and Lord of Chatenay,
PRINCE DE CELLAMERE, the Spanish Am-
    bassador,
MARÉCHAL DE VILLEROY,
MADEMOISELLE SOPHIE DE LAUNAY,
COMTE DE LAVAL,
JOSEPH DE LAGRANGE-CHANCEL, a satirical
    poet,
M. DE SAINT-GENEST, a poet,
ABBÉ DE CHAULIEU,
M. DE SAINT-AULAIRE,
M. ANTOINE DE CHASTELLUX,
MADAME LA MARÉCHALE DE VILLEROY,
MADAME DE CHANOST,
MADAME DE BRISSAC,
MADAME DE ROHAN,
MADAME DE CROISSY,
D'AVRANCHES, valet-de-chambre to Madame
    du Maine,
ABBÉ BRIGAUD,
M. DE BESSAC, an ensign in the Guards of
    Duc du Maine,
CHEVALIER RAOUL D'HARMENTAL, in love
    with Bathilde,
BARON RENÉ DE VALEF, his friend,

conspirators against the Regent.

CAUCHEREAU, a tenor of the Académie Royal, favorite of
Mademoiselle de Chartres.

MONSIEUR DE RIOM, favorite of La Duchesse de Berri.

MADEMOISELLE BURY, of the Opera.

ALBERT DU ROCHER, an officer in the service of Duc d'Orléans.

CLARICE DU ROCHER, his wife.

BATHILDE, their daughter, in love with the Chevalier d'Harmental.

JEAN BUVAT, an employee in the government library.

MONSIEUR DUCONDRAY, his colleague.

NANETTE, Bathilde's servant.

MAÎTRE DURAND, a restaurant-keeper.

RAFFÉ, valet-de-chambre to M. le Duc de Richelieu.

BOURGUINON, } in the service of the Abbé Dubois.
COMTOIS,

MADAME DENIS, a lodging-house keeper.

MADEMOISELLE ÉMILIE, } her daughters.
MADEMOISELLE ATHENAISE,

BONIFACE DENIS, her son.

MONSIEUR FREMOND, a lodger at the house of Madame Denis.

LA FILLON.

LA NORMANDIE.

CAPTAIN ROQUEFINETTE, an adventurer.

THE REGENT'S DAUGHTER.

INTRODUCTORY NOTE.

WHEN the Conspiracy of Cellamare, which forms
the main theme of the "Chevalier d'Harmental,"
was exposed, or when the Abbé Dubois thought
fit to put an end to it, the Duchesse du Maine
was condemned by the regent to undergo imprisonment in the Château of Dijon. In due course of
time her longing to renew the glories of her own
little court at Sceaux made her enforced sojourn
in the provinces extremely irksome to her, and she
purchased her liberty by making a full disclosure
of the names of all who had been cognizant of, or
privy to, the negotiations with Alberoni, as representing the Court of Spain. It thus became known
to the authorities that the main reliance of the
conspirators for active support had been the province of Bretagne. These disclosures threw much
light upon certain symptoms of disaffection which
had appeared in that province, whose people seemed
almost to form a race apart from those of other

portions of the kingdom. It turned out that the resistance of the States of Bretagne to the orders of the royal governor was but a cover for continued negotiations with Spain, looking toward a permanent separation of Bretagne from France. The States at last declared the province independent because its privileges had been invaded; and the standard of rebellion was thus boldly displayed. The progress and crisis of the revolt are described with sufficient fidelity to truth in these pages. The name of Gaston de Chanlay is the only one of the five which has no place in an absolutely accurate record of the scene in the public square of Nantes, at midnight of a certain tempestuous night in March, 1720.

"To this day," says Dumas, in one of his strictly historical works, " La Regence," " in the very heart of Bretagne, at Saint-Malo, at Lorient, at Villeneuve, at Brest or Finisterre, one finds in the poorest huts portraits of Talhouet, Pontcalec, Mont-louis, and Du Couëdic handed down from father to son. And when you ask your hosts, the occupants of these huts, who these men are whose features they preserve so devoutly, in their trustful ignorance some will reply: 'They are saints;' others, 'They are martyrs.'"

The scenes between the regent and Dubois are

particularly interesting, because they mark so sharply the contrast between the regent's natural disposition to leniency and mercy—even, perhaps most of all, to those whose blows were aimed at his own person or power—and the facility with which he yielded to the representations of his mentor, whose hold upon his mind and will grew stronger day by day until the end.

The Duc d'Orléans has been fortunate in this, that the virtues which he did possess—large-hearted generosity, unfailing kindness and courtesy to his inferiors, and intense affection for his children, whether born in or out of wedlock—have seldom failed to arouse emotions distinctly resembling sympathy for one whose vices, though of monumental proportions, were those of the age in which he lived, and whose life was embittered by cruel, unmerited accusations of having caused the untimely deaths of the Duc and Duchesse de Bourgogne and the Duc de Bretagne,—the father, mother, and brother of the young king. It is always to be remembered to his credit that he watched with unfailing care and affection over the well-being of the royal child, whose hold upon life was always feeble and uncertain, and who alone stood between him and what was still one of the most exalted thrones of Christendom.

The regent was not fortunate in his legitimate daughters. The career of the Duchesse de Berri is revolting and saddening in the extreme, even although we are told by one of the contemporary memoir-writers that a *post-mortem* examination revealed the fact that she was "crack-brained." The convent life of the Abbess of Chelles was little short of scandalous; while the matrimonial bickerings of Mademoiselle de Valois and her husband, the Duke of Modena, were of European notoriety. A fourth daughter became the wife of the Prince of Asturias, and was Queen of Spain for the few months which intervened between the absurd abdication of Philippe V. and the death of her husband. Her leading characteristics were an extremely morose disposition, and personal habits slovenly in the extreme; and her Spanish subjects seized the first convenient pretext to send her back to France, and were very remiss in remitting her allowance. The youngest of all, Mademoiselle de Beaujolais, was the only one who combined good morals with an attractive personality, and she died of a broken heart almost before she was out of her teens.

The memoirs of Madame de Staal-de Launay furnish abundant authority for the entertaining description given by Dumas of the life led by

the conspirators in the Bastille. The author of
the memoirs was decidedly heartless in her treatment of poor Maison-Rouge, the lieutenant of the
fortress, whose ardent passion for herself she pitilessly used as a means of forwarding her love
affair with the Chevalier de Mesnil. The following
passage is illustrative of the skill with which she
kept two strings to her bow; and at the same time
it enlightens us still further as to the diversions
in which these fortunate prisoners were allowed
to indulge.

"One day when he (Maison-Rouge) was taking
supper with me, Mesnil, who had found a way of
opening the door of his room, came and listened
at my door. He claimed that I was very gay and
lively, and that I had spoken of him with insulting
levity. But he was even more put out because,
when we left the table, we went to the window,
the weather being extremely warm. There the
lieutenant suggested that I should sing, and I
began a scene from the opera of "Iphigénie."
The Duc de Richelieu, who was at his window,
sang the reply of Orestes, which fitted in very
nicely with our situation. Maison-Rouge, who
thought that it entertained me, allowed us to
sing the scene through. It was by no means
entertaining to the Chevalier de Mesnil. The

next day he questioned me in his letter about the
supper, at which I had no idea that he had been
a listener. I did not remember that his name
had been mentioned between us, so I said nothing
about it to him. This seemed to him to import
some secret understanding between Maison-Rouge
and myself, and he was so enraged that he insisted
upon my breaking with the lieutenant. I at last
succeeded, however, in making him understand how
excessively inconvenient that would be for our
affairs, and he cooled down."

Messire Voyer d'Argenson, an excellent lieutenant of police transformed into a very mediocre
keeper of the seals, subjected Mademoiselle de
Launay to an inquisitory ordeal very similar to
that undergone at his hands by Gaston de Chanlay;
and the versatile *femme de chambre* acquitted herself with no less skill and discretion than was
exhibited by the Breton hero. M. d'Argenson is
an interesting figure of the period, no less in his
own right than as the father of two sons, each
of whom made an honorable name in high office
under Louis XV. The Marquis owes his greatest
fame, however, to his very entertaining and valuable memoirs of the first thirty years of the reign.

When Madame du Maine was at last allowed
to return to Sceaux, she found assembled there,

Pompadour, Laval, Malezieux, and Mademoiselle de Launay. "Waiting," says Dumas, "to recommence those delightful entertainments which poor, blind Chaulieu, who could not see them, used to call "*les nuits blanches de Sceaux.*"

It is, perhaps, mere supererogation to repeat what has been said so often of others of M. Dumas' romances, — that contemporary authority can be cited for every anecdote or incident not directly connected with the distinctively romantic portions of the narrative.

The Princess Palatine's pleasantry as to the gifts of the fairies to her son at his birth is told by Saint-Simon and Duclos, as is the anecdote of the same out-spoken lady's very forcible expression of her displeasure when her son's contemplated marriage was announced to her. Saint-Simon, again, and the Marquis d'Argenson agree in affirming that Dubois had the temerity to demand a nomination to the Sacred College from Louis XIV. as a reward for his potent assistance in bringing about that marriage. This latter anecdote is discredited, however, by a very recent writer,[1] who has undertaken, with what measure of success it does not concern us to inquire, to clear away some

[1] James Breck Perkins, in "France Under the Regency," etc.

of the odium with which Dubois has been surrounded from his death to the present day.

The assumption of queenly pomp by the mad Duchesse de Berri, as well as her secret marriage with Riom, are equally well authenticated. The wrath of the Princess Palatine at this misalliance was far more violent than that of the culprit's father, who certainly was indulgent to a fault. The severity with which Riom was treated was due to the outcry of the grandmother, rather than to the outraged dignity of the father.

There is, alas, no doubt that the regent's daily avocations and distractions are faithfully described in the course of this narrative. Saint-Simon, his chief apologist, deplores the fact which he cannot explain away, except by putting the blame upon the shoulders of Dubois; but the generous impulse to which D'Orléans is made to yield when he pardons De Chanlay, whose avowed object was to compass his death, is no less characteristic of the unfortunate prince, of whom the same apologist, who was also his dearest friend, said long after his death that his character was an enigma which he had never been able to solve.

THE REGENT'S DAUGHTER.

LIST OF CHARACTERS.

Period, 1719.

PHILIPPE, DUC D'ORLÉANS, Regent of France.
MADAME ELIZABETH CHARLOTTE, PRINCESS PALATINE, his
    mother.
DUCHESSE D'ORLÉANS, his wife.
DUCHESSE DE BERRI,
MADEMOISELLE DE CHARTRES, Abbess of Chelles, } daughters of
MADEMOISELLE DE VALOIS, the Regent.
LOUIS, the Regent's son.
ABBÉ DUBOIS, Minister of State.
HÉLÈNE DE CHAVERNY, a natural daughter of the Regent, in
    love with Gaston de Chanlay.
DUC DE ST. SIMON,
MARQUIS DE BROGLIE,
DUC DE NOAILLES, } of the French Court.
CHEVALIER DE SIMIANE,
M. DE BIRON,
M. DE MOUCHY,
MARQUIS DE LAFARE, Captain of the Regent's Guards.
MARQUIS DE LA VRILLIÈRE, } of the Council.
M. DE LEBLANC,
MESSIRE VOYER D'ARGENSON, Lieutenant of Police

M. DE LAUNAY, Governor of the Bastille.

M. DE MAISON-ROUGE, his Lieutenant.

DUC DE RICHELIEU,
MARQUIS DE POMPADOUR,
COMTE DE LAVAL,
M. DE MALEZIEUX,   } prisoners in the Bastille.
ABBÉ BRIGAUD,
CHEVALIER DUMESNIL,
MADEMOISELLE SOPHIE DE LAUNAY,

CAUCHEREAU, music-master to Mademoiselle de Chartres.

CHEVALIER DE RIOM, married to Duchesse de Berri.

COMTE DE NOCÉ, a friend of the Regent.

CARDINAL ALBERONI.

DUC D'OLIVARÈS, a Spanish agent.

GASTON DE CHANLAY, in love with Hélène,
MARQUIS DE PONTCALEC,
M. DE MONTLOUIS,   } conspirators against the Regent's life.
M. DU COUËDIC,
M. DE TALHOUET,
CAPTAIN LA JONQUIÈRE,

MARQUIS DE GUER, uncle of Marquis de Pontcalec.

SIRE DE PONTCALEC.

THE SORCERESS OF SAVÉNAY.

BARON DE CARADEC.

M. DE MONTARAU, intendent of the Province of Bretagne.

MARÉCHAL DE MONTESQUIOU, commanding at Bretagne.

M. DE CHATEAUNEUF.

LA SOURIS, the Regent's favorite.

JULIE, the mistress of Dubois.

CHEVALIER DE M——.

MADAME URSULE, Superior of the Ursulines at Clisson.

SISTER THÉRÈSE, of the Ursulines.

MADAME DESROCHES, in the Regent's Service.

BOURGUIGNON, landlord of the Hôtel "Muid d'Amour."

LA JONCIÈRE, a smuggler.

LA JONQUILLE, sergeant in the French Guards.

GRIPPART,
L'ENLEVANT, } soldiers.

OVEN, Gaston de Chanlay's servant.

TAPIN,
L'ÉVEILLÉ, } in the service of Dubois.

CHRISTOPHER, a jailer at Nantes.

LAMER, the executioner.

MEMOIRS OF A PHYSICIAN.

INTRODUCTORY NOTE.

THE leading events of the last years of the long
and disastrous reign of Louis XV. are described in
these volumes with the author's accustomed accuracy and fulness of detail. During those years
the unhappy kingdom of France seems to have
taken its longest strides towards the end which
keen observers had long seen to be inevitable.

In "Olympe de Clèves" we have seen the king,
young, handsome, and flattered, hesitating on the
threshold of the career of debauchery into which
his intriguing courtiers, with the assent if not the
co-operation of the all-powerful minister and former preceptor, Fleury, were striving to force him
for their own selfish ends. In these Memoirs of
Balsamo, we are shown the deplorable close of that
career half a century later. During that half-
century — the "period of the Decadence of the
Monarchy," it has been called by Monsieur Henri
Martin — the people of France, groaning beneath
the weight of extortion and oppression, had seen

the prevailing luxury and extravagance of the court increase in proportion as their own burdens grew. Rapacious mistresses, each with her following of greedy sycophants and relatives, had succeeded one another with scarcely a breathing space between; costly and disastrous wars had been waged to gratify their whims or to avenge real or fancied slights put upon them. Small wonder that he who had been greeted on his return from the brilliant but unproductive victory of Fontenoy with the title of Louis le Bien-Aimé (the Well-beloved), had come to be the most hated and despised man in the realm.

It is interesting to observe the steady degeneration (if we may use the word) in social standing of the successive favorites of Louis XV.

The three sisters De Nesle — Madame de Mailly, Madame de Vintimille, and the Duchesse de Chateauroux — were scions of one of the most venerable families in France, and could trace their lineage back to the twelfth century. To be sure their immediate progenitors were of decidedly unsavory character, but such considerations were of slight importance to a generation which was the direct heir of the traditions of the Regency. To Madame de Chateauroux succeeded Jeanne Antoinette Poisson, daughter of a commissary's clerk, and wife of a rich farmer-general's nephew and heir,—that is to say, a typical representative of the bourgeoisie, or middle, class. For twenty years this minister in petticoats, created Marquise de Pompadour, ruled the kingdom of France over the shoulders of its weak and dissolute monarch. That she was utterly unscrupulous as to the means she employed to maintain her ascendency, the infamous invention of the *Parc aux Cerfs* is, in itself, sufficient proof.

Frederick the Great sneeringly called her "Cotillon II.;" but Maria Theresa wrote her a letter in which she called her "my dear cousin." So small a matter as this decided the policy of France at a critical period: Madame de Pompadour declared in favor of alliance with Austria, the "Seven Years' War" ensued, and France was despoiled of her colonial possessions, and left practically helpless at the mercy of her enemies.

She it was who "made" Choiseul, and established his influence and authority upon so firm a foundation that her death left him the supreme power in the kingdom. Past experience had taught the lesson that he could be dislodged in no other way than by the accession of a new favorite, and any hopes which may have arisen in the hearts of those who really desired to see an end of the regime of shame and scandal which had endured so long, were destined to be short-lived.

The versions of the story are so numerous and conflicting that it is impossible — and perhaps unimportant — to say with certainty who is entitled to the doubtful honor of having brought about the first meeting between the king and the young woman whose career under the name of the Comtesse du Barry is one of the most remarkable in history. There is no doubt, however, as to the antecedents of the young woman in question, or that when Louis XV. raised her to the shameful eminence which Madame de Pompadour had last occupied, he reached the lowest point in the social scale, and selected a true daughter of the people.

She was born in the little provincial town of Vaucouleurs in 1743, and was the illegitimate child of one Anne Bécu. Her early history may be read in many places; nowhere perhaps is it told more concisely or interestingly than by MM. de Goncourt (in " La du Barry "). Being thrown entirely on her own resources in the streets of Paris, whither her mother had been driven by poverty, possessed of extraordinary personal attractions, and with very lax ideas on the subject of female virtue, her story is not an edifying one. She fell at last into the hands of Comte Jean du Barry, a native of Toulouse who had lived many years at Paris, and whose career of heedless, cynical, and unbridled licentiousness and debauchery — noteworthy, even in those days — had won for him the title of *the* Roué. She had meanwhile taken the name of Rauçon, — her mother having married one of that name, — and had subsequently adopted the *nom-de-guerre* of Mademoiselle Lange.

The attachment between the blasé comte and the beautiful courtesan soon became one of interest solely, and as it came to Du Barry's knowledge that the enemies of the Duc de Choiseul were seeking to fill the void which Madame de Pompadour's death had left in the king's affections, he conceived the idea of putting forward La Lange as a fit candidate.

In some way or other the agency of Lebel, the king's confidential valet, was made use of, and the discarded mistress of the Roué was placed where the eye of royalty would fall upon her. There seems to have been little thought, except in the mind of Du Barry, that the result would be anything more than the passing fancy of a day; but the impression made by the clever creature was not only immediate, but gave such indubitable signs of having come to stay that Lebel " was alarmed at the unworthy attachment which seemed to have taken full possession of the king's mind and heart. He

informed his master that the woman who had been
brought to his notice was unmarried, and untitled,
and he thought it his duty to call the king's attention to the compromising results of any further acquaintance with her. The king stopped him short,
told him to arrange a marriage for her at once, and,
when she was married, to bring her to Compiègne."
(De Goncourt.)

It is probable that Richelieu, the ever young,
whom we have seen in the "Chevalier d'Harmental" and the "Regent's Daughter," in the far-off
days of the regency while the king was yet in his
cradle, already a past master in gallantry, and adding zest to his amatory pursuits by playing the part
of Harlequin in the burlesque called the "Conspiracy of Cellamare," and again, in "Olympe de
Clèves," with diplomatic honors thick upon him,
devoting his energies to the corruption of his youthful sovereign, — it is probable, we say, that Richelieu
was instrumental in bringing Mademoiselle Lange to
the king's notice. Throughout the reign of Louis XV.
this mock-conspirator, mock-soldier, and mock-states-
man, who never appeared in his true colors except
as a libertine and dabbler in petty intrigues, was
always at the ear of the king, pandering to the
tastes which he had done more than any other to
form, and fawning upon the favorite of the day,

her subservient slave, — the king's evil genuis, in very truth.

The picture of the cynical, heartless old rake drawn by Dumas is one of the best of the many admirable ones presented in these pages.

To return to the new favorite. Comte Jean du Barry had a convenient brother, Guillaume, at Toulouse, who readily consented to a marriage which required him to make no sacrifice of his liberty, and provided a handsome allowance for his complaisance. A false registry of the bride's baptism was manufactured, in which her birth was put back three years to 1746, and she was represented to have been born in wedlock of Anne Bécu, by her husband, one Jean Jacques Gomard de Vaubernier. The banns were published, the marriage ceremony was performed, the groom returned to Toulouse, and the bride went at once to Versailles, where she was installed in the apartments lately occupied by the king's daughter, Madame Adelaide.

Nothing need be added to Dumas's masterly delineation of Madame du Barry's character and conduct. There were very few among the great ladies of the court whose horror at the spectacle of a woman picked up from the street to be placed over all their heads did not soon yield to the necessity of being well with her. She brought

to Versailles the manners and the slang of the local-
ities in which her life had been passed; but it is
only fair to say that she showed such marvellous
power to adapt herself to her new surroundings
that it may safely be assumed that her lapses into
the slang of the brothel were intentional, because
she found that they amused the king. De Goncourt relates that a continuous run of ill-luck at
the card-table drew from her the ejaculation, *"Ah !
je suis frite !"* (I am fried.) "We are bound to believe you, Madame," replied an ill-natured wit, gath-
ering in her stakes, "for you certainly ought to
know." This by way of allusion to the profes-
sion of her mother, who was cook to a celebrated
courtesan.

It is difficult to give any idea of the sums squan-
dered by Madame du Barry during her reign, except by copious extracts from the voluminous documents detailing those sums which are deposited in
the "Bibliothèque Nationale." While she had not
the same longing for acquisitions of real property
which characterized Madame de Pompadour, she
more than made up for it by her purchases of
dresses and jewelry, pictures, sculpture, and the
like, the total of which amounted to many hun-
dreds of millions of francs. Few queens, indeed,
have ever been able to boast of such a collection of

jewels as those which were stolen from the favorite on the 10th of January, 1791, — a theft which led to her four voyages to England, and the consequent accusations of emigration and of secret missions to the foes of the Republic.

There is in the "Bibliothèque Nationale" a manuscript journal, written by one Hardy, a Parisian of the middle class, called " Journal des évènements tels qu'ils parviennent à ma connaissance " (Journal of such facts as have come to my knowledge). The following is one of the many entertaining bits of gossip to be found therein. He says that a clerical friend of his was dining out on the 1st of February, 1769, and was requested by a brother of the cloth to drink "to the presentation." Hardy's friend failed to understand what he meant, and asked if he referred to the Presentation of our Lord at the Temple, which was to be commemorated the following day. "No," said the priest who proposed the toast, "I refer to that which will take place to-day, if it did not come off yesterday — the presentation of the new Esther, who is to supersede Haman, and rescue the people of Israel from captivity." The new Esther was Madame du Barry, and Haman, the Duc de Choiseul, in this allegory.

Indeed, the breathless interest excited by this important function, which gave to the mere mistress the more stable character of favorite *en titre*, can hardly be exaggerated. "Du Barry had unearthed a Comtesse de Béarn," says De Goncourt, " the widow of a Perigord gentleman, who had left her in very necessitous circumstances, with five children on her hands, and a venerable lawsuit against the Saluces family. He obtained for her an allowance which made it possible for her to appear at Court in garb suited to her position, and procured a judgment favorable to her in her lawsuit, thereby making sure of a sponsor." Even then, however, the function was delayed on one pretext or another: " the Comtesse de Béarn, dreading the effect of her complaisance upon her future, at one time pretended that she had sprained her ankle, and obstinately kept to her sofa for some days; " and it was not until the 21st of April, 1769, that the long-looked-for presentation took place. The delay which occurred at the last moment is historical; it was caused by the delinquency of a hair-dresser.

Choiseul, the bosom friend and confident of Madame de Pompadour, could have been influenced by no virtuous scruples in refusing to live on terms of friendship with Madame du Barry. He trusted too much to his established position, and to the need which the king had of him, and rejected the innumerable advances which were made to him on the part of the favorite, of whom it must be said that politics was as uncongenial a field of activity to her as it was a congenial one to Madame de Pompadour. She desired to be friendly to the Minister, and it was his overweening self-confidence which drove her into the opposite faction, and made her the tool of those who were opposed to all that Choiseul represented. A strange sight it was to see the woman of the street put forward by the party of the devotees, — their real object being to reinstate the Jesuits whom Madame de Pompadour had driven out of France. Even the stern ascetic Christophe de Beaumont, Archbishop of Paris, juggled with his conscience to avoid offending the favorite when Louis was on his death-bed.

Choiseul, on the other hand, was the representative of the philosophers, the obstreperous Parliament, and the Jansenists. In his exile at Chanteloupe he was visited by vast numbers of his adherents, and the greatest and noblest names in the kingdom were inscribed upon the pillars there. "People were not more virtuous," says Saint Amand, "but opposition was fashionable."

It may be said of Marie Antoinette, as of Choiseul, that the enmity between herself and the favorite was not the fault of the latter. It would not perhaps be surprising that the daughter of the

Cæsars should have disdained the lowly-born courtesan, were it not that in so doing she was running
directly counter to the wishes and commands of
her mother, the politic Maria Theresa. The correspondence of the Empress with Mercy-Argenteau,
her representative at the French Court, is copiously
cited by Saint Amand (Les Dernières Années de
Louis XV.). It is filled with emphatic expressions
of the necessity of her daughter's bowing to circumstances, and showing her respect for the king by
courteous treatment of *those whom he loves.*

It is, perhaps, needless to say that " Chon " is a
very real personage. She was Mademoiselle Claire
du Barry, sister of Comte Jean ; she was a great favorite of her sister-in-law, and the guiding spirit of
the household.

Zamore, too, the little toy negro, was actually
made governor of Luciennes, and received the
emoluments pertaining to the governorship of a
royal chateau. It is not, however, as governor of
Luciennes that he won his most enduring fame,
but as the serpent who turned upon his benefactress
and rent her asunder.

When Louis XV. was dead of the smallpox,
Madame du Barry was exiled ; but it was only a
short time before Luciennes was restored to her by
the good-natured successor of her royal lover, and

there she lived until the Revolution, during the last
years of tranquillity the very dearly loved mistress
of the Duc de Cossé-Brissac.   In 1791 her jewels
were stolen, and she unwisely called public attention to the fact of her great wealth by offering a
reward of two thousand louis for their recovery.
The thieves were arrested in England, and she was
compelled to make four journeys across the channel
before she was able to recover them.   The story of
the accusations made against her, as a sequel of
those voyages, is too long to be told here.   All her
servants turned against her, and none more vindic-
tively than Zamore, who had become a zealous
republican.   On the 8th of December, 1793, she
ascended the scaffold, and " looked through the little window of la Guillotine," just fifty-three days
after the unhappy queen had lost her life on the
same spot.   " The death of Madame du Barry cost
the conscience of the Terror a quarter of an hour
more than that of Marie Antoinette," says De Goncourt.   " It took the jury an hour and a quarter to
convict in the case of the favorite."

The "affair of La Chalotais," which is mentioned so frequently in connection with the Duc
d'Aiguillon, arose out of the latter's incumbency of
the office of military commandant of Bretagne, during one of the periodical revolts of the parliament

of that restless province, which he had put down
with great severity. The English made a descent
upon the coast of Bretagne in 1758; D'Aiguillon
defeated them at Saint-Cast, and drove them aboard
their ships, but the Bretons claimed that the Duc
was not entitled to any credit personally, and
accused him of hiding in a mill.

Some one remarked in the presence of Monsieur de
la Chalotais that " Monsieur d'Aiguillon covered himself with glory at the battle of Saint-Cast."

" With flour you mean," replied La Chalotais, who
was procureur-général of the parliament of Bretagne.

D'Aiguillon never forgave it, and seized the first
opportunity to prosecute La Chalotais for an alleged
plot to overthrow the monarchy. He was imprisoned, and became at once the idol of the parliament, and eventually D'Aiguillon was replaced by
Duc de Duras.

Guiseppe Balsamo, better known to fame as the
Count Cagliostro, under which name he appears in the
other romances of the Marie Antoinette cycle, was a
charlatan of extraordinary ability who made a great
stir in various European countries during the last
quarter of the eighteenth century. In his hands
free-masonry, which was then under the ban, became
a very powerful weapon, and he was much aided in
making dupes by his wife Lorenza Feliciani, a

woman of rare beauty, who was also a member of the masonic fraternity. At one time or another he seems to have claimed to possess most of the powers which are here ascribed to him, and which he attributed to the supernatural connections of his master, Althotas, or Alhotas. His name is known in French history for his relations with the Cardinal de Rohan, and his consequent connection with the wretched affair of the necklace, which is the subject of the second of this series of romances.

It will, perhaps, be more convenient to speak of Marie Antoinette at length, in connection with that episode which occurred after she had become queen, and had begun to develop those traits of character which came to the surface so many times, and wrecked so many apparent opportunities of making peace with the Revolution. In this story we see little of her that is not sweet and lovable. Without the gloomy predictions of Balsamo, she might well shudder at the succession of evil omens which welcomed her to France. The apartment which was prepared for her reception on the island in the Rhine where her Austrian escort delivered her to the representatives of her adopted country, was hung with tapestries representing the legend of Jason, Medea, and Crœsus. For this fact we have no less an authority than Goethe, who was then a student at Strasbourg; his reflections upon the impropriety of such decoration under the circumstances were no less just than forcible.

The fearful storm which interfered with the celebration at Versailles was fittingly capped by the horrible slaughter in Paris the following night, which is so graphically described by Dumas. The Dauphiness was driving into Paris for the first time to see the illuminations, when she was met by intelligence of the disaster, and drove sadly back to Versailles.

To one who has studied Rousseau in his own " Confessions," the glimpses of the testy, suspicious old *philosophe* are by no means the least attractive portions of the book.

Although this story closes with the death of Louis XV., fifteen years before the taking of the Bastille, the introduction of Marat, the gloomy and repulsive fanatic, and above all his reappearance on the last page, give a distinct forecast of what the future had in store.

MEMOIRS OF A PHYSICIAN.

LIST OF CHARACTERS.

Period, 1770 to 1774.

Louis XV., King of France.

Marie Jeanne de Vaubernier, Comtesse Dubarry, his mistress.

Louis Auguste, Duc de Berry, the Dauphin, afterwards Louis XVI.,
Comte d'Artois,
Comte de Provence,
} grandsons of the King.

Princess Louise de France,
Princess Adélaïde,
Princess Victoire,
Princess Sophie,
} daughters of Louis XV.

Duc de Chartres, afterwards Philippe Égalité, Duc d'Orléans.

Duc de Choiseul, Prime Minister of France.

Maria Theresa, Empress of Austria.

Marie Antoinette, Archduchess of Austria and Dauphiness of France.

Duc de la Vauguyon, tutor of the royal princes.

Comte de Coigny, gentleman-in-waiting to the Dauphin.

The Countess of Langershausen, waiting on Marie Antoinette.

Comte de Stainville, brother-in-law of M. de Choiseul and Governor of Strasbourg.

Cardinal Louis de Rohan.

MARÉCHAL DE RICHELIEU,
DUC D'AIGUILLON, his nephew, M. de
    Choiseul's successor,
M. DE FRONSAC, Richelieu's son,
PRINCE DE SOUBISE,
MARÉCHAL DE LUXEMBOURG,
PRINCE DE GUÉMÉNÉE,   gentlemen of the
PRINCE DE CONDÉ,   French Court.
COMTE DE LA VAUDRAYE,
M. D'ALAMBERT,
M. DE MALESHERBES,
DUC DE LA VRILLIÈRE,
DUC DE TESMES, a hunchback,

DUCHESSE DE CHOISEUL,
DUCHESSE DE GRAMMONT, M. de Choiseul's sister,
PRINCESSE DE GUÉMÉNÉE,
COMTESSE D'EGMONT, Richelieu's daughter,
MARQUISE DE MIREPOIX,   ladies of the
DUCHESSE D'AYEN,   French
BARONNE D'ALOGNY,   Court.
DUCHESSE DE NOAILLES,
MARQUISE DE SAVIGNY,
MADAME D'EPINAY,
MADAME DE POLASTRON,
COMTE DE SARTINES, Lieutenant of Police.
LA FOUINE, his clerk.
M. DE SÉGUIER, Advocate-General.
M. BIGNON, Provost of the Merchants.
M. DE LA CHALOTAIS, Attorney-General.
M. DE PRASLIN, of the Choiseul ministry.
M. DE BERTIN, } of the Aiguillon ministry.
ABBÉ TERRAY, }
M. DE MAUPEOU, Vice-Chancellor.
M. DE BOYNES, of the Parliament.
MONSIEUR RÉMY, Vicar of St. Johns, Strasburg.

BARON JOSEPH BALSAMO, otherwise known as Acharat and Comte de Fenix, afterwards Cagliostro.

LORENZA FELICIANI, his wife.

ALTHOTAS, a philosopher.

EMMANUEL SWEDENBORG,
JOHN PAUL JONES,
LORD FAIRFAX,
SCIEFFORT, a Russian, } chiefs of a secret brotherhood.
XIMENES, a Spaniard,
JOHN CASPER LAVATER,
JEAN PAUL MARAT,

BARON DE TAVERNEY MAISON ROUGE.

CLAIRE ANDRÉE DE TAVERNEY, his daughter.

CHEVALIER PHILIPPE DE TAVERNEY MAISON ROUGE, Andrée's brother.

NICOLE LEGAY, Andrée's waiting-maid.

GILBERT, a poor youth, in love with Andrée.

LA BRIE, servant of Baron de Taverney.

JEAN JACQUES ROUSSEAU,
M. DE VOLTAIRE,
M. CARON DE BEAUMARCHAIS,
M. DE HOLBACH, } writers in the reign of Louis XV.
M. DE LA HARPE,
M. DIDEROT,
MARMONTEL,

M. DE JUSSIEU, botanist.

M. BOUCHER, painter.

M. PIGALE, sculptor.

CHEVALIER DE MUY.

M. MIQUE, the King's architect.

MONSIEUR LOUIS, Marie Antoinette's physician.

MONSIEUR BORDEU,
MONSIEUR LA MARTINIÈRE, } physicians to Louis XV.

ANASTASIE EUPHÉMIE RODOLPHE, Comtesse de Béarn.

MAÎTRE FLAGEOT, her lawyer.

MARGUERITE, his servant.

CHONCHON, sister of Madame Dubarry.

VICOMTE JEAN DUBARRY.

ZAMORE, Comtesse Dubarry's negro page.

MADEMOISELLE SYLVIE, } Comtesse Dubarry's maids.
MADEMOISELLE DORÉE,

SEBASTIAN, a courier in the service of Madame de Grammont.

M. DE BEAUSIRE, Nicole Legay's lover.

M. LUBIN, court hairdresser.

MADAME LUBIN.

LEBEL, valet to Louis XV.

RAFTÉ, Richelieu's secretary.

M. GRANGE, an intendent.

MAÎTRE NIQUET, a notary.

MAÎTRE GUILDOU, an attorney.

THÉRÈSE, Rousseau's wife.

FRITZ, Balsamo's servant.

MARGUERITE, servant of Andrée de Taverney.

M. LÉONARD, a hairdresser.

COMTOIS, a coachman.

COURTIN, a postilion.

DAME GRIVETTE, Marat's servant.

HAVARD, a patient at the Hôtel Dieu Hospital.

M. GUILLOTIN, M.D.

SIMON, a shoemaker's apprentice.

PITOU, a peasant of VILLERS-COTTERET.

MADELEINE PITOU, his wife.

ANGE PITOU, their son.

ANGÉLIQUE, Pitou's sister.

CAPTAIN OF THE "ADONIS."

THE QUEEN'S NECKLACE.

INTRODUCTORY NOTE.

A CRUEL fate seemed to have ordained that from the moment that Louis XVI. and his lovely Austrian queen ascended the throne of France, the worst possible construction should be placed upon their every act, however innocent or well-meant in itself. The verdict of all investigators into the proximate causes and the course of the French Revolution — of all, that is, who can fairly make any claim to impartiality, and their name is legion — is so nearly unanimous that it has come to be a mere truism, that the unhappy king and queen were the victims of the time in which they lived; that they reaped the harvest sown by their predecessors, and that the greatest crime that can be attributed to them is lack of judgment, — a failure to appreciate and acquiesce in the inevitable trend of events.

Says Carlyle, in his essay on the " Diamond Necklace," apostrophizing Marie Antoinette : —

"Thy fault in the French Revolution was that thou wert the Symbol of the Sin and Misery of a thousand years; that with St. Bartholomew and Jacqueries, with Gabelles and Dragonnades and Parcs-aux-Cerfs, the heart of mankind was filled full, and foamed over into all-involving madness. . . . As poor peasants, how happy, worthy had ye two been! But by evil destiny ye were made a King and Queen of; and so both once more — are become an astonishment and a byword to all times."

The wrong note was struck when Louis XVI. in the first days of his reign, professing, and honestly without doubt, a purpose to institute useful reforms, and to avoid the scandals which had disgraced the closing years of his grandfather's reign, went back half a century for his Prime Minister, and unearthed the Comte de Maurepas, who had been in retirement since he was forced out of office by Madame de Pompadour, thirty years before. We can read in many places — for instance, in the "Mémoires" of the Comte de Ségur, the friend of Lafayette — the unfortunate impression that was produced by this reversion to the reactionary ideas of the last generation. The wrong note was struck, and yet it turned out to be the key-note of all that was to follow.

Let us glance now for a moment at the first occasion given by Marie Antoinette for unfriendly criticism after she became queen. It has been described by Madame Campan, the queen's first lady-in-waiting.

It seems that the new king and queen received visits of condolence on the death of Louis XV. at La Muette, and were condoled with by a large assemblage, composed in great part of venerable dowagers with marvellous constructions in the way of head-gear, which made some of them " appear somewhat ridiculous." But the queen's dignity was equal to the occasion, and " she was not guilty of the grave fault of laying aside the state she was bound to preserve," although the kittenish behavior of one of her *dames du palais* laid her open to the charge of doing so. The Marquise de Clermont-Tonnerre, tired of standing, as her functions required, sat down on the floor, " behind the fence formed by the hoops of the queen and her ladies." There she amused herself by " twitching the dresses of the ladies, and a thousand other tricks." The queen was moved to laughter, and several times placed her fan before her face to hide her smiles, to the intense wrath of the elderly females present, who attributed her amusement to their appearance. The inevitable *chanson* appeared next day. Madame Campan remembered only the chorus, which ran thus, —

"Little Queen, you must not be
So saucy with your twenty years :
Your ill-used courtiers soon will see
You pass once more the barriers.
                    Fal lal la, fal lal la."

"More than fifteen years after this," says Madame Campan, "I heard some old ladies, in the most retired part of Auvergne, relating all the particulars of the day of public condolence for the late king, on which, as they said, the queen had laughed in the faces of the sexagenarian duchesses and princesses who had thought it their duty to appear on the occasion."

This incident is given at length because it is typical of the whole experience of the poor queen, whose every act and every word was perverted, and with the assistance, it must be said, of her own bad judgment and the king's, on almost every occasion was made to serve as a nail in the coffin of her popularity.

Madame Campan's pages are full of similar episodes, trivial in appearance, but really, as seen in the light of subsequent events, possessing a sinister significance. If the effects of Madame de Clermont-Tonnerre's playfulness lasted fifteen years, we may easily understand that the wretched affair which forms the groundwork of the romance contained in these volumes had much wider and more far-reaching consequences than, taken by itself, it would seem to merit.

It should be said that the crisis of this affair of the necklace (" Affaire du Collier ") came directly upon the heels of the first performances of the much discussed " Mariage de Figaro " of Beaumarchais. It had been kept off the stage for some time by the king's order, on account of divers Voltairean and levelling doctrines enunciated in it, and was finally produced, substantially unchanged, by virtue of a permit granted with the understanding that the objectionable passages had been stricken out. It was received with such thunders of applause that the king did not venture to stop it; but the author was imprisoned, and public opinion was very outspoken.

With regard to the actual facts concerning the famous necklace, it may be said, first, that they are largely shrouded in impenetrable mystery, and, secondly, that, so far as they can be deciphered with any certainty, they substantially agree with the version given by Dumas.

The materials for unravelling the very tangled thread are voluminous, consisting largely of the absolutely inconsistent statements made by the various defendants, and which form part of the records of the trial. There is also a life of Madame de La Motte written by herself; a letter from London from the pen of Cagliostro; the memoirs of Abbé Georgel, private secretary of Cardinal de Rohan, and Madame Campan. But the most important evidence — indeed, the only really important evidence — was burned up by Abbé Georgel, in obedience to the note written by Rohan at the time of his arrest, which reached him before seals were put upon the Cardinal's papers. Other presumably damnatory documents were destroyed by Madame de La Motte before her arrest. All the existing evidence Carlyle claims, and undoubtedly with perfect truth, to have sifted and weighed carefully; and his conclusions demonstrate the impossibility of ever coming at the whole truth as to the proper apportionment of responsibility between La Motte and Rohan.

The only approach to accurate information as to the date when the necklace was put together is the statement of Madame Campan that it was originally intended for Madame du Barry, who "went into half pay"[1] in 1774, when Louis XV. died.

To the dismay of Boehmer, Marie Antoinette refused to consider the purchase of the necklace. "We have more need of seventy-fours than of

[1] Carlyle.

Necklaces," she said. For three years after that, it was hawked around among the crowned heads of Europe, but to no purpose. "The age of Chivalry is gone, and that of Bankruptcy is come." Among others, "the Portuguese Ambassador praises, but will not purchase."

At last, one day, poor Boehmer, who, as Court Jeweller, had some peculiar privileges, bursts into the queen's apartment, flings himself at her Majesty's feet, and entreats her either to buy his necklace, or give him permission to drown himself in the Seine. She coolly suggests that he might, as a possible third course, take the necklace to pieces, and dismisses him.

The foundation of the queen's dislike, almost hatred, of Cardinal de Rohan, seems to have had its origin in a despatch sent by him while he was Ambassador at Vienna, to this effect: "Maria Theresa stands, indeed, with the handkerchief in one hand, weeping for the woes of Poland; but with the sword in the other hand, ready to cut Poland in sections and take her share." D'Aiguillon, who was then minister, communicates the letter to Louis XV., and he to Du Barry, "to season her *souper*." It became a court-joke, and got to the ears of the Dauphiness, who never forgot it.

If, as seems very doubtful, the Cardinal did speak disparagingly of the princess to her mother, he must have repented it in sackcloth and ashes, for there seems to be no question as to the reality of his passion for her, dating from his return to France soon after the death of Louis XV. "Through ten long years," says Carlyle, " of new resolve and new despondency, of flying from Saverne to Paris and from Paris to Saverne, has it lasted; hope deferred making the heart sick." Meanwhile he had secured the Archbishopric (of Strasburg), the Grand Almonership, the Cardinalship, "and lastly, to appease the Jews, that fattest Commendatorship, founded by King Thierri, the Do-nothing. . . . 'All good!' languidly croaks Rohan; 'yet all not the one thing needful: alas, the queen's eyes do not yet shine on me.'

"Abbé Georgel admits, in his own polite diplomatic way, that the Mud-volcano [Rohan] was much agitated by these trials; and in time quite changed. Monseigneur deviated into cabalistic courses, after elixirs, philters, and the philosopher's stone; that is, the volcanic steam grew thicker and heavier; at last, by Cagliostro's magic (for Cagliostro and the Cardinal by elective affinity must meet), it sank into the opacity of perfect London fog."

It is said that Guiseppe or "Beppo" Balsamo, otherwise Count Alessandro di Cagliostro, in his younger days took some pains to procure from a country vicar, under the falsest of pretences, "a bit of cotton steeped in holy oils." This seemingly insignificant circumstance is given much importance by Carlyle, in his extremely searching and thorough analysis of this remarkable character, as tending to prove that there was at the bottom of his nature "a certain musk-grain of real superstitious belief." It must be said, however, that history affords but slight justification for endowing him with any of the nobler qualities which are attributed to him in these pages. From the very beginning of his career as a *gamin* in the streets of Palermo, where he was born in 1743, down to his death in prison at Rome fifty-odd years later, he seldom failed to exhibit all the distinctive traits of an impostor and a charlatan. His claim, so often touched upon by Dumas, that he had lived for several thousand years, is well illustrated by the historical fact that he was wont, when passing a statue of Christ, "to pause with a wondrously accented plaintive 'Ha!' as of recognition, as of thousand years' remembrance."

It will be remembered that, in the introduction to the "Memoirs of a Physician," Dumas mentions the Swiss Lavater as one of the prominent actors in the mystic assemblage on Mont Tonnerre. The association between the two really existed; and the impression made by the pupil of Althotas upon the worthy and learned savant is a convincing proof of his marvellous power of imposition. Lavater said of him: —

" Cagliostro — a man such as few are; in whom, however, I am not a believer. Oh that he were simple of heart and humble, like a child; that he had feeling for the simplicity of the gospel and the majesty of the Lord! Who were so great as he? Cagliostro often tells what is not true, and promises what he does not perform. *Yet do I nowise hold his operations as deception*, though they are not what he calls them."

The problems presented by the unexampled career of this man were grappled with by Schiller, giving rise to his unfinished novel of the " Geisterseher; " and by Goethe, who relieved his mind from the hold the matter took upon it by writing the drama called the " Gross-Kophta." After wandering many years through many lands, Cagliostro found at Strasburg " the richest, inflammablest, most open-handed dupe ever yet vouchsafed him," in the person of the Prince-Cardinal Louis de Rohan, of whom the Abbé Georgel wrote that " he came at last to have no other will than Cagliostro's."

His connection with the affair of the necklace is rather problematical, except in so far as he was the confidant and mystical adviser of the Cardinal, whose hopes, founded upon his supposed correspondence with the queen, he undoubtedly nursed with his predictions of great power and influence to come by means of it.

The early history of Jeanne de Saint-Remy, by courtesy Countess, styled also of Valois, is told by Dumas with substantial accuracy, and need not be repeated here.

She married Monsieur de La Motte, a private in the Gendarmes, at Bar-sur-Aube, and dubbed him Count, by virtue of her own Countess-ship.

In 1783 she first met Rohan at Saverne, whither she went with Madame de Boulainvilliers; and there and then, so far as the workings of her ingenious mind can be followed, she seems to have formed the outline of the scheme which developed into the barefaced deception of Rohan, and the theft of the necklace.

For eighteen months after the scheme had taken shape in her brain, she carried on the fictitious correspondence with the Cardinal, assisted by Retau de Villette, an associate of her husband, " in the subterranean shades of rascaldom," and finally ventured upon the audacious deception, in which Dumas makes

Nicole Oliva Legay figure as her accomplice. That part, however, was really played by a Parisian courtesan named Essigny, known to history under the name of Gay d'Oliva, or Olisva, which was given her by La Motte, the latter form being an anagram of *Valois*.

If Madame Campan is to be credited, Marie Antoinette had never seen Madame de La Motte, but the Countess had once met one Desclos, a valet of the queen's bed-chamber, at the house of a surgeon at Versailles. This Desclos figured prominently in the deception put upon the Cardinal; for Retau de Villette personated him, or is supposed to have done so, on several momentous occasions when the Countess found it necessary to produce a duly accredited agent of the queen.

Thus, then, a bargain is arranged between Boehmer, still with a necklace for sale, and " Madame Lamotte de Saint-Remy de Saint-Shifty," as representing Monsieur de Rohan. On the 1st of February, 1785, the famous jewel was delivered to the Cardinal, who signed a receipt for it : by him it was handed over to the Countess at Versailles for transmission to the queen. A knock is heard at the door, and Monseigneur retires to an alcove whence he can see what takes place. Enters valet Desclos, alias Retau de Villette, who receives the precious casket, with solemn injunctions and promises, and retires. "Thus softly, silently, like a very dream, flits away our solid necklace, — through the Horn Gate of Dreams."

It was taken to pieces and sold under the auspices of "Count" de La Motte, in London and elsewhere, long before the explosion.

Let us now listen for a moment to Madame Campan, as she relates the circumstances under which the explosion took place. Her narrative naïvely displays the almost incredible lack of judgment on the part of the queen, who, while she was undoubtedly free from any guilt in the transaction, seemed fated to act as if she were guilty. It will be noticed that the alleged signature of the queen, "Marie Antoinette de *France*," was in the possession of the Cardinal, and that it was made a subject of accusation against him that he should not have recognized the impossibility of the queen's having so designated herself : —

"When Madame Sophie was born, the queen told me that Monsieur de Sainte-James, a rich financier, had apprised her that Boehmer was still intent upon the sale of his necklace, and that she ought, for her own satisfaction, to endeavor to learn what the man had done with it: she desired me, the first time I should meet him, to speak with him about it, as if from the interest I took in his welfare. I did so, and he told me he had been fortunate enough to sell it at Constantinople for the favorite Sultana. I told the queen, who was delighted to hear it, but could not understand how the Sultan came to purchase his diamonds in Paris.

"She long avoided seeing Boehmer, being fearful of his rash character.

"On the baptism of the Duc d'Angoulême in 1785, the king gave him a diamond epaulette and buckles, and directed Boehmer to deliver them to the queen. He presented them on her return from mass, and at the same time handed her a letter in the form of a petition. In this he told her that he was happy to see her 'in possession of the finest diamonds in Europe,' and begged her not to forget him. The queen read the letter aloud, and saw nothing in it but a proof of mental aberration; she lighted the paper at a wax taper standing near her, as she had some letters to seal, saying, 'It is not worth keeping.' She afterwards much regretted the loss of this enigmatical memorial.

.   .   .   .

"On the 3d of August Boehmer came to me at my country house at Crespy [the first payment was to be made July 30th, but, of course, was not]. He was extremely uneasy at not having received any answer from the queen, and asked me if I had no commission for him. I told him no. . . . 'But,' said Boehmer, 'the

answer to the letter I handed her — to whom must
I apply for that?' 'To nobody,' I answered; 'the
queen burned it without understanding it.' 'Ah!
Madame,' he exclaimed, 'that is impossible; the queen
knows that she has money to pay me !' "

He then proceeded to inform her that the queen
wanted the necklace, and had had it purchased for
her by Cardinal de Rohan.

"'You are deceived,' I exclaimed; 'the queen has
not once spoken to the Cardinal since his return from
Vienna: there is not a man at Court less favorably
looked upon.' 'You are deceived yourself, Madame,'
said Boehmer; 'she sees him so much in private that
it was to him she gave thirty thousand francs, which
were paid me as an instalment : she took them in his
presence out of the little secrétaire of Sèvres porcelain,
next the fireplace in her room.' 'And the Cardinal
told you all this?' 'Yes, Madame, himself.' 'What
a detestable plot!' I cried. 'Indeed, Madame, I begin to be much alarmed, for his Eminence assured me
that the queen would wear the necklace on Whit-Sun-
day; but I did not see it upon her, and that was why I
wrote to her Majesty.'

. . . .

"Boehmer never said one word to me about the
woman Lamotte, and her name was mentioned for the
first time by the Cardinal in his answers to the inter-
rogatories put to him before the king."

Boehmer subsequently had an interview with the queen, after he had reported to the Cardinal the result of his conversation with Madame Campan. He related to her all that he had been made to believe had taken place between her and himself through the medium of the Cardinal. He refused to listen to her denials, and kept repeating : " Madame, the time for pretending has gone by : condescend to confess that you have my necklace, and let some assistance be given me, or my bankruptcy will soon bring everything to light."

It was after this interview that the queen told the Baron de Breteuil the whole story. He was, as is well known, an inveterate enemy of Rohan, and was only too glad of the opportunity to disgrace him.

" On the following Sunday, the 15th August, being the Assumption, at twelve o'clock, at the very moment when the Cardinal, dressed in his pontifical garments, was about to proceed to the chapel, he was sent for to the king's closet where the queen was."

He was then questioned by the king, admitted that he had been duped, and produced the alleged letter from the queen, signed " Marie Antoinette de France," and offered to pay for the necklace himself. He became much confused, and made contradictory statements, and was at last given into custody, but was able, as stated above, to provide for the destruction of his papers, whereby an impenetrable cloud was thrown over the whole affair. He was followed to the Bastille by Madame de La Motte and her husband, Cagliostro, Retau de Villette, and Mademoiselle Gay d'Oliva. The trial dragged through many weary months, during which unheard-of efforts were made by the family of the Cardinal as well as the clergy, even to the Pope himself, to procure for him the right to be tried at Rome. "The conduct of the king and queen," says Madame Campan, "was equally and loudly censured in the apartments of Versailles, and in the hôtels and coffee-houses of Paris." This was because they did not hush the matter up. What would have been said, had they tried to do so?

On the 31st of May, 1786, "at nine in the evening, after a sitting of eighteen hours," the Parliament of Paris solemnly pronounced judgment: —

Cardinal de Rohan goes scot-free: "Countess de Lamotte is shaven on the head, branded with red-hot iron V (*Voleuse*) on both shoulders, and confined for life to the Salpetrière; her Count wandering uncertain, with diamonds for sale, over the British Empire; the Sieur de Villette, for handling a queen's pen, is banished forever; the too queenlike Demoiselle Gay d'Oliva (with her unfathered infant) 'put out of Court:' and Grand Cophta Cagliostro, liberated indeed, but pillaged, and ordered forthwith to take himself away."

The king, persisting in his view that the Cardinal and the woman La Motte were equally culpable, sought to restore the balance of justice by exiling the Cardinal to La-Chaise-Dieu, and suffering Madame de La Motte to escape a few days after her incarceration, thus confirming Paris in the opinion that the latter had really interested the queen herself.

"Thus," says Carlyle, "does the miserable pickle-herring tragedy of the Diamond Necklace wind itself up."

Of the romantic as distinguished from the historical portions of the " Queen's Necklace " little need be said, save that one has not far to seek in French history of the last century to find precedents in profusion for the unpaternal conduct of the elder Taverney. Andrée and Philippe are still struggling against the cruel fate which seems to have doomed them to know no part of life but its sorrows; while we are introduced for the first time to Olivier de Charny, of whom we are to see much more in the later volumes of this cycle.

To the historical characters of the story we must add Beausire, who is thus mentioned in a manuscript note to the collection of documents published under the title of " Affaire du Collier " : —

" Gay d'Oliva got married some years afterward to one Beausire, an ex-noble, formerly attached to the D'Artois household. In 1790 he was Captain of the National Guard Company of the Temple. He then retired to Choisy, and managed to be named Procureur of that Commune; he finally employed himself in drawing up lists of proscription in the Luxembourg Prison, where he played the part of informer."

Him also, and Nicole or Oliva, we shall meet again.

Once more, as the story closes, we are reminded by the apparition of the ghoul-like Marat, accompanied by the more human Robespierre, of the gradual approach of the cataclysm.

In the volumes which succeed we shall find them no longer hovering on the outskirts of the crowd, but taking a too prominent part in the world, — shaping events which are there chronicled.

THE QUEEN'S NECKLACE.

LIST OF CHARACTERS.

Period, 1784–1785.

Louis XVI., King of France.

Marie Antoinette, his Queen.

Comte de Provence,
Comte d'Artois, } brothers of the King.

Comtesse d'Artois.

Duc d'Angoulême, son of Comte d'Artois.

Duc d'Orléans.

Princesse de Lamballe.

The Princess Royal.

Gustavus, King of Sweden, visiting Richelieu under the assumed name of Comte de Haga.

Prince Louis, Cardinal de Rohan, Grand Almoner of France.

M. de Calonne, Minister of Finance.

Baron de Breteuil, Keeper of the Seals.

Maréchal de Castries, Minister of the Navy.

M. de Lapeyrouse, a navigator.

Maréchal de Richelieu.

Comtesse Dubarry.

Comte de Launay, Governor of the Bastille.

M. de Crosne, Lieutenant of Police.

Marquis de Favras, Captain of the Guards of Comte de Provence.

Marquis de Lafayette.

Comte Cagliostro.

Jeanne de Saint-Rémy Valois, Comtesse de La Motte.

Comte de La Motte.

M. Doillot, Madame de La Motte's counsel.

Admiral de Suffren.

Comte Olivier de Charny, his nephew,
Chevalier Philippe de Taverney Maison } in love with the
Rouge,   Queen.

Andrée de Taverney, maid-of-honor to Marie Antoinette.

Baron de Taverney Maison Rouge.

Mademoiselle Oliva, formerly called Nicole Legay.

M. de Beausire, her lover.

Toussaint, son of Beausire and Oliva.

Manoel, a Portuguese adventurer.

M. Boehmer, } jewellers, in possession of the diamond necklace.
M. Bossange, }

Retau de Vilette, a journalist.

Abbé Lékel, Almoner of the Bastille.

M. de Suza, the Portuguese Ambassador.

M. Ducorneau, Chancellor of the Portuguese Embassy.

M. Caron de Beaumarchais, dramatic writer.

M. Necker.

Doctor Mesmer.

Doctor Deslon, a disciple of Mesmer.

M. de Bergasse, one of Mesmer's patients.

Saint-Martin, teacher of spiritualism.

Maximilien de Robespierre.

Jean Paul Marat.

M. Breton, Clerk of the Court judging Madame de La Motte.

Marquis de Condorcet,
Comte de Coigny,
M. de Lauzun,
M. de Vaudreuil,
M. de Condé,   } of the French Court.
M. de Trémouille,
M. de Penthièvre,
Baron de Planta,
Madame de Polignac,

MADAME DUVAL, lady-in-waiting to Marie Antoinette.
MADAME DE MISERY, first lady of the bed-chamber.
MADAME PATRIX, lady's maid to the Queen.
DR. LOUIS, the Queen's physician.
WEBER, Marie Antoinette's coachman.
M. LÉONARD, her hairdresser.
LAURENT, a porter at the palace.
M. LENOIR, an architect.
THE MAJOR-DOMO OF MARÉCHAL DE RICHELIEU.
CLOTILDE, Madame de La Motte's servant.
ALDEGONDE, Retau de Vilette's servant.
M. FINGRET, a Paris upholsterer.
LANDRY, RÉMY, and SYLVAIN, his apprentices.
HUBERT, a keeper at the Bastille.
MADAME HUBERT, his wife.
SAINT-GEORGES, a skater.
GUYON, a turnkey at the Bastille.

ANGE PITOU.

INTRODUCTORY NOTE.

ON Christmas Day, 1753, Lord Chesterfield wrote from Paris, summing up his observations on the state of France : " In short, all the symptoms which I have ever met with in history, previous to great changes and revolutions in government, now exist and daily increase in France."

This, being written so early and by a foreigner, is perhaps the most noteworthy of the prophecies of disaster to come which were trumpeted forth by so many keen-sighted intellects during the last half of the eighteenth century.   It was floating in the air ; it was written upon the faces of the starving, down-trodden people, who found themselves burdened with this tax and that tax, with tithes and *tailles*, from which the nobility and clergy were exempt ; while on the other hand, the luxury and extravagance of those privileged classes grew every day more wanton, and their vices more shameless.   Upon such a foundation the philosophers and encyclopædists had built solidly and well, so that Voltaire wrote exultingly of the "glorious sights" which the young men of his day would live to see; wherefore they were greatly to be envied!

The old Marquis de Mirabeau, father of him who became so prominent a figure during the early months of the Revolution, — a curious, crabbed old fellow, who called himself the "friend of men," and whose peculiarities are described by Dumas in the "Comtesse de Charny," — wrote in his memoirs a description of a peasant's holiday which he witnessed in the provinces about the time of the death of Louis XV. (1774). After describing the dance which ended in a battle, and "the frightful men, or rather frightful wild animals, . . . of gigantic stature, heightened by high wooden clogs, . . . their faces haggard and covered with long greasy hair, — the upper part of the visage waxing pale, the lower, distorting itself into the attempt at a cruel laugh and a sort of ferocious impatience," — he moralizes thus: "And these people pay the *taille!* And you want, further, to take their salt from them! And you know not what it is you are stripping barer, or as you call it, governing, — what, by a spurt of your pen, in its cold, dastard indifference, you will fancy you can starve always with impunity, always till the catastrophe come! Ah, Madame, such government by blindman's-buff, stumbling along too far, will end in a general overturn."

It is curious to notice with what unanimity the good intentions of Louis XVI. are admitted, almost taken for granted, by all writers upon this period, except the virulent pamphleteers of the day. Even Michelet admits it, though somewhat grudgingly,— Michelet, who went out of his way to charge Louis XV., whose load of sin was heavy enough in all conscience, with a foul crime for which there seems to be no shadow of authority.

But it is hard to convince one's self that the general overturn could have been avoided, even had the will and character of the young king been as worthy of praise as his impulses and intentions undoubtedly were. Hastened it was, beyond question, by his weakness at critical moments, by his subserviency to the will of the queen, which was exerted uninterruptedly, and with what now seems like fatal perversity, in the wrong direction, during the years when there was still a chance, at least, of saving the monarchy. It was through the influence of the queen and her intimate circle that step after step, which, if taken in time, would have made a favorable impression upon an impressionable people, "whose nature it was to love their kings," was delayed until it was, so to say, extorted, and hence bereft of all appearance of a willing, voluntary concession. Numerous instances of this fatality, if we may so call it, are told by Dumas; notably the day's postponement of the king's journey to Paris after the day of the Bastille.

With the virtuous, philosophic Turgot, "who had a whole reformed France in his head," for Controller-General of the Finances, the reign of Louis XVI. seemed to start off under the best of auspices. But, as Carlyle tersely puts it, "Turgot has faculties, honesty, insight, heroic volition, but the Fortunatus's purse he has not. Sanguine controller-general! a whole pacific French Revolution may stand schemed in the head of the thinker, but who shall pay the unspeakable 'indemnities' that will be needed? Alas! far from that; on the very threshold of the business he proposes that the clergy, the *noblesse*, the very parliaments, be subjected to taxes like the people! One shriek of indignation and astonishment reverberates through all the château galleries; . . . the poor king, who had written to him a few weeks ago, 'You and I are the only ones who have the people's interest at heart,' must write now a dismissal, and let the French Revolution accomplish itself, pacifically or not, as it can."

To Turgot succeeded Necker, also a skilful and honest financier, also with schemes of peaceful reform in his head. For five years he carried the burden; and at last he, too, was driven to propose the taxation of clergy and nobility, and thereupon to take his departure, May, 1781.

Under the short administrations of Joly de Fleury and D'Ormesson, matters failed to improve (as indeed, how could they do otherwise?), until on the retirement of the latter, when the king purchased Rambouillet, without consulting him, in the autumn of 1783, "matters threaten to come to a still-stand," says Carlyle.

At such a crisis destiny decreed that M. de Calonne should be put forward to fill the vacancy, — a man of indisputable genius, "before all things, for borrowing."

"Hope radiates from his face, persuasion hangs on his tongue. For all straits he has present remedy, and will make the world roll on wheels before him."

In the "Diamond Necklace," Dumas has given us a faithful picture of Calonne and his method of exploiting his financial genius. His grandiloquent, "Madame, if it is but difficult, it is done; if it is impossible, it shall be done," seems hardly to stamp him as the man for the place at that critical period,

however great may have been the felicity of the
Œil-de-Bœuf under the temporary plenty which resulted from the policy of "borrowing at any price."

It would be hard to exaggerate the effect upon
the growing aspirations of the French people after
the unfamiliar something which they came to call
"liberty," of the result of the struggle in America,
in which the cause of the colonists was so powerfully supported by the little band of Frenchmen of
whom Lafayette was the most prominent and the
most notable. He returned to France in 1783, to
be dubbed in some quarters "Scipio Americanus."

The scandalous affair of the necklace was, as we
have heretofore seen, seized upon by the enemies of
the queen as a weapon with which to assail her
reputation, although her absolute innocence of any
guilty connection with it is now beyond doubt.
The results of this unfortunate episode — the "immense rumor and conjecture from all mankind,"
coupled with the slanderous charges made by
Madame Lamotte in a letter from London after
her escape from the Salpétrière — went far towards
creating the unreasoning hatred of the "Austrian
woman," which she herself did so little to assuage
when the clouds became blacker than night, and
began to emit the thunder and lightning of the
Revolution.

In the spring of 1787, Calonne, his borrowing powers being at an end, conceived the idea of convoking the "Notables"—an expedient unheard of for one hundred and sixty years—to sanction his new plan of taxation. They met on the 22d of February, 1787, one hundred and thirty-seven of them, "men of the sword, men of the robe, peers, dignified clergy, parliamentary presidents," with seven princes of the blood to preside over the seven *bureaux*,—"a round gross in all." They would have none of Calonne or his plans; and he was dismissed in April, after which the "Notables" sat until May 25, "treating of all manner of public things," and then first were the States-General mentioned.

Calonne was succeeded by Cardinal Loménie de Brienne,—a dissolute, worthless sexagenarian, who devised various tax-edicts, stamp-taxes, and the like, all of which the Parliament of Paris refused to register. The expedient of a Bed of Justice was resorted to, and resulted in the most ominous of all portents: for the first time in history the Parliament refused to obey the royal "Je veux" (I wish it.) They were exiled for a month,—August to September, 1787,—and returned upon conditions.

In the spring of 1788, Loménie's great scheme of dismissing the parliaments altogether, and substituting a more subservient "Plenary Court" was detected before it was ripe, and denounced to the Parliament of Paris, which body, upon remonstrating, was again exiled (May). An attempt thereafter to raise supplies by royal edict simply, led to the rebellion of all the provincial parliaments, the public expressing its approval more noisily than ever. On August 8 appeared a royal edict to the effect that the States-General should be convoked for May following; it was followed by another edict, that treasury payments should thenceforth be made three-fifths in cash and two-fifths in paper, — a virtual confession that the treasury was insolvent. Thereupon Loménie was incontinently dismissed, and Necker recalled from Switzerland to become the "Savior of France."

A second convocation of the "Notables" (November 6 to December 12, 1788) undertook to decide how the States should be held: whether the three estates should meet as one deliberative body, or as three, or two; and, most important of all, what should be the relative force, in voting, of the Third Estate, or Commonalty. They separated without settling any of the points in question.

In January, 1789, the elections began, — the real beginning of the French Revolution in the opinion of Carlyle, and indeed, of most writers.

On the 13th of July, 1788, there had been a
most destructive hail-storm throughout France, and
the growing crops were literally destroyed; whereby the extreme destitution which had come to be
the natural condition of the lower classes had been
accentuated. In addition, the winter of 1788–89
was one of extreme rigor, so that it seemed almost
as if God himself were openly manifesting his will
that the general overturn should come.

The riot in which Réveillon, the paper manufac-
turer, was concerned occurred in April, 1789, just
prior to the assembling of the States-General on
May 4.

The clergy and nobility at once exhibited their
purpose to act as separate bodies; and the Third
Estate, led by Mirabeau and others, decided that it
must be the mainspring of the whole, and that it
would remain "inert" until the other two estates
should join with it; under which circumstances it
could outvote them and do what it chose. For
seven weeks this state of "inertia" endured, until
the court decided to intervene and the assembly
hall was found closed against the representatives of
the people on June 20. Thereupon they met in
the old tennis-court (Jeu de Paume), and there the
celebrated "Oath of the Tennis-Court" was taken by
every man of them but one, — an oath "that they

will not separate for man below, but will meet in all places, under all circumstances, wheresoever two or three can get together, till they have made the Constitution."

One subsequent attempt was made by the king to intimidate this ominously persistent body; but the messenger whom he despatched to command them to separate ("Mercury" de Brézé, Carlyle calls him) was addressed in very plain language by the lion-headed Mirabeau, and retired in confusion. The court recoiled before the spectacle of "all France on the edge of blazing out;" the other two estates joined the Third, which triumphed in every particular. Henceforth the States-General are the "National Assembly," sometimes called the "Constituent Assembly," or assembly met to make the constitution.

This cursory sketch of the leading events of the early years of the reign of Louis XVI. is offered as a sort of supplement to that presented by Dumas before he takes his readers into the "thick of the business" in Paris.

The badly veiled military preparations to which the terror of the queen and the court led the king to consent, kept the Parisian populace in a constant state of fermentation, which was powerfully helped on by the continued scarcity of food and the consequent influx of starving provincials into the metropolis. The Gardes Françaises gave indubitable symptoms of popular leanings, which perhaps emboldened the effervescent spirits of the mob more than a little.

The news of the dismissal of Necker, circulated on Sunday, July 12, kindled the first panic terror of Paris into a wild frenzy, and resulted in the siege of the Bastille, "perhaps the most momentous known to history."

The course of events immediately preceding the descent upon that "stronghold of tyranny, called Bastille, or 'building,' as if there were no other building," as well as those of the siege itself, is traced with marvellous fidelity by Dumas, due allowance being made, of course, for the necessities of the romance. He closely follows Michelet; but the details are told, with substantial unanimity, by all historians of the fateful event.

The part assigned to Billot in the narrative before us was in reality played by several persons. It was Thuriot, an elector from the Hôtel de Ville, who gained admission to the fortress and investigated its condition; who ascended with De Launay to the battlements and showed himself to the mob to quiet their fears that he had been foully dealt with. This same Thuriot, as president of the convention, refused to allow Robespierre to speak in

his own defence on the 10th Thermidor, year II.
(July 28, 1794). It was Louis Tournay, a black-
smith and old soldier of the Regiment Dauphiné,
who hacked away the chain which upheld the first
drawbridge. It was an unknown man who first
essayed to cross the ditch to take the note dictating
terms and fell to the bottom (and was killed); but
it was Stanislas Maillard who followed and made
the passage in safety.

Élie and Hullin, it is needless to say, are historical characters, and worthy of an honorable place
in history for their heroic attempts, then and afterwards, to prevent the needless shedding of blood.

The extraordinary thing about the attack on the
Bastille is the startling unanimity of the people
that it was the first and fittest object of attack. It
seems the more extraordinary because, as Michelet
has said, it "was by no means reasonable;" for the
lower orders had suffered but little from imprisonment in the Bastille.

"Nobody proposed, but all believed and all
acted. Along the streets, the quays, the bridges,
and the boulevards, the crowd shouted to the crowd:
'To the Bastille! The Bastille!' And the tolling
of the tocsin sounded in every ear: *à la Bastille!*

"Nobody, I repeat, gave the impulse. The ora-
tors of the Palais Royal passed the time in drawing

up a list of proscriptions, in condemning the queen to death, as well as Madame de Polignac, Artois, Flesselles, the provost, and others. The names of the conquerors of the Bastille do not include one of these makers of motions."

Perhaps we may accept, in the absence of a better, Michelet's explanation of this instinctive action of the mob, as having been caused by the recent publicity given to the experience of one Latude, who was first confined in the Bastille during the reign of Madame de Pompadour, and had since "worn out all their prisons," and had finally reached the "dunghills of Bicêtre," by way of Vincennes and Charenton. He was at last released through the pertinacious efforts of one Madame Legros, a poor mercer, who became interested in him by chance, and persevered for three years, meeting with obstacles of every sort and exposed to the vilest calumny, until success came at last, and Latude was released in 1784, after more than forty years of confinement. His release was followed by an ordinance enjoining intendants never again to incarcerate anybody at the request of families *without a well-grounded reason*, and in every case *to indicate the duration of confinement*, — a decidedly naïve confession of the degree of arbitrariness which had been reached.

"From that day" (of Latude's deliverance), says Michelet, "the people of the town and the faubourg, who, in that much-frequented quarter, were ever passing and repassing in its shadow, never failed to curse it."

It is proper to observe that the state of things which existed in the Bastille when the Cellamare conspirators underwent mock imprisonment there (witness the Regency Romances) had been done away with. While other prisons had become more merciful, this had become more cruel. From reign to reign the privileges were taken away, the windows were walled up one after another, and new bars were added. The other encroachments by De Launay upon the "liberties of the Bastille" are described by Dumas in the course of the narrative.

To quote Michelet once more: "The Bastille was known and detested by the whole world. 'Bastille' and 'tyranny' were in every language synonymous terms. Every nation, at the news of its destruction, believed it had recovered its liberty."

The Comte de Ségur, then ambassador at Russia, relates that when the news arrived in St. Petersburg, men of every nation were to be seen shouting and weeping in the streets, and repeating, as they embraced one another: "Who can help weeping for joy? The Bastille is taken!"

The Duc de Liancourt announced the fall of the fortress to Louis XVI. "Why," said the king, "it is downright revolt!" "It's more than that," replied Liancourt, "it is revolution."

Nothing need be added to the description given by Dumas of the painful excitement at Versailles, or of the king's journey to Paris and experience there. The scenes attending the summary vengeance wreaked upon Foulon and Berthier, who were the very incarnation of the old régime, are also portrayed with the careful attention to detail which is so striking a characteristic of the historical portions of the author's romances; and the same may be said of the assassination of Flesselles, and, by anticipation, of the events of the 5th of October in the streets of Paris and at the Hôtel de Ville, when Stanislas Maillard assumed the leadership of the women ("the Menadic hosts"), and Lafayette was reluctantly compelled to lead the march of the thirty thousand upon Versailles.

The fall of the Bastille was followed throughout France by the enlistment of National Guards, ostensibly, in most instances, as a protection against mythical brigands, whose coming in great numbers was continually heralded in every town and village, but who never came. The experience of Pitou, in Haramont, is typical of the great movement which was in progress everywhere.

"It is a terrible but certain fact," says Michelet, "that in Paris, that city of eight hundred thousand souls, there was no public authority for the space of three months, from July to October."

Meanwhile the National Assembly was going haltingly on with its work of constitution-making. The session of the 4th of August shines out with peculiar prominence, as it was the occasion of all the privileged classes vying with one another in renouncing their privileges. Such good effect as this tardy renunciation might have had, however, was destroyed by the king's refusal to sanction it, except in so far as he was personally affected.

Towards the end of August the knotty question of the veto was duly reached: whether the king should have any veto upon the acts of the Assembly, and if so, whether it should be absolute or suspensive.

Throughout Lafayette assumed a position of great prominence in other directions than as commander-in-chief of the National Guard. The "suspensive" veto was finally decided upon, and there was a vague prospect of a return of quieter times, except for the continued scarcity and dearness of grain. "Our rights of man are voted," says Carlyle; "feudalism and all tyranny abolished; yet behold we stand in queue [at the bakers' doors]! Is it aristocrat forestallers — a court still bent on intrigue? Something is rotten somewhere."

With hope, terror, suspicion, excitement, succeeding one another with bewildering rapidity, comes the certainty that the "Œil-de-Bœuf is rallying," that the Flanders regiment has been summoned to Versailles, and that some scheme of flight or repression is in the wind. Then comes the news of the banquet of the 1st of October, — of the appearance of the king and queen, the trampling under foot of cockades, and the announcement of Marie Antoinette the next day, that she was "enchanted with the events of the supper." Of all fatuous performances of mortals foredoomed to destroy themselves, surely that was the most fatuous. It is significant, by the way, of the extreme caution with which the statements of Madame Campan must be accepted, that in describing this scene, at which she was present, she does not mention the word "cockade," nor does she imply that it was aught but a quiet, orderly function, at which, perhaps, some one or two may have imbibed a thought too freely.

With regard to the events of the night of October 5–6 at Versailles, nothing need be said, save that the body-guard who heroically defended the door to the queen's apartments, where Georges de Charny is said to have been slain, was one

Miomandre de Sainte-Marie; and that although "fractured, slashed, lacerated, left for dead, he has crawled to the Œil-de-Bœuf, and shall live honored of loyal France."

In the "Comtesse de Charny" we shall find the king and queen on the road to Paris, on the 6th of October. We shall there meet many old acquaintances and make some new ones, and shall follow the setting sun of the time-honored monarchy of France till it sinks at last below the horizon.

ANGE PITOU.

LIST OF CHARACTERS.

Period, 1789.

Louis XVI., King of France.
Marie Antoinette.
Comte d'Artois,
Comte de Provence, } the King's brothers.
Princesse de Lamballe.
The Dauphin.
Madame Royale.
Louis Philippe Joseph, Duc d'Orléans, afterwards Philippe
    Égalité.
M. de Calonne, Comptroller-General.
M. de Crosme, Lieutenant of police.
Comte de Launay, Governor of the Bastile.
Comtesse Jules de Polignac, favorite of the Queen.
Diane, Duchesse de Polignac, her sister-in-law.
Madame Campan, waiting-woman to the Queen.
Madame de Tourzel, governess of the royal children.
Marquis de Lafayette, Commander-in-Chief of the National
    Guards of France,
Baron de Necker.
Madame de Staël, his daughter.
M. Turgot.
Madame Hagué,
Madame Thibault, } attending on the Queen.
Comte Olivier de Charny, Lieutenant of the Queen's Guards.
Andrée de Taverney, Comtesse de Charny.

BARON GEORGE DE CHARNY,
VICOMTE ISIDOR DE CHARNY, } brothers of Comte de Charny.

PRINCE DE BEAUVAU,
M. DE VILLEROY,
M. DE NESLE, } gentlemen of the King's household.
M. DE VILLEQUIER,

PRINCE DE CONDÉ,
PRINCE DE LAMBESQ,
MARÉCHAL DE BROGLIE,
COMTE D'ESTAING,
M. DE DREUX BRÉZÉ,
BARON DE BESENVAL, } officers commanding the Royal Troops.
M. DE NARBONNE FRITZJAR,
M. DE SALKENAYM,
M. DE BIRON,
M. DE LUSIGNAN,

M. DE PERSEVAL, aide-de-camp of Comte d'Estaing.

M. DE CLERMONT-TONNERE,
M. DE SARTINE,
MARIE DE LAVAL, } friends of Marie Antoinette.
MADAME DE MAGNEVILLE,
M. DE COIGNY,

BARON DE BRETEUIL,
M. DE LA ROCHEFOUCAULT,
COMTE DE MAUREPAS, } of the French Court.
COMTE DE MACHAUT,
M. DE BRIENNE,
M. DE VARICOURT,

CHEVALIER D'ABZAC, Chief of the Royal Stable.

COUNT CAGLIOSTRO.

DR. HONORÉ GILBERT.

SEBASTIEN GILBERT, his son.

ABBÉ FORTIER, a schoolmaster.

LOUIS ANGE PITOU, one of his pupils, afterwards Commander of the National Guard of Haramout.

Rose Angélique Pitou, Pitou's aunt.

Billot, a farmer of Villers-Cotteret, afterwards leading the attack on the Bastille.

Catherine, his daughter.

Madame Billot.

Camille Desmoulins,
Jean Paul Marat,
Stanislaus Maillard, an usher of the Châtelet Court, } Revolutionists.
Madeleine Chambry, a flower-girl,
Verrière, a deformed dwarf,
Danton,

Élie, formerly an officer in the Queen's regiment,
Hullin, a chasseur, } taking part in the attack on the Bastille.
Gonchon, the "Mirabeau of the People,"
Arne, Challot, and de Lepine, soldiers,

Gabriel Honoré Mirabeau,
M. de Sièyes, } members of the National Assembly.
M. Guillotin, M.D.,
M. Monnier,

M. de Flesselles, Provost of the Merchants of Paris.

M. de Bailly, his successor.

M. de Saint-Priest, minister for Paris.

M. de Foulon.

M. Berthier de Sauvigny, his son-in-law.

Saint-Jean, Foulon's servant.

M. Rappe, syndic.

M. Delavigne, President of the Electors.

M. Rivière, an Elector.

M. Acloque, President of the St. Marcel District.

Abbé Lefèvre d'Ormesson.

Abbé Delille.

Abbé Maury.

Abbé Béradier, Principal of the College of Louis-le-Grand.

Doctor Mesmer.

M. de Losme, Major of the Bastille.

Réveillon, a paper-manufacturer.

Master Farollet, tennis-master-in-chief to Duc d'Orléans.

Pasdeloup, a police agent.

Captain Goudran, of the National Guard.

Sergeant Rigold.

M. Cornu, a hatter.

M. Dulauroy, a tailor.

Father Clovis, a hermit.

M. Furth, a pamphleteer.

Father Lefranc, a farmer.

M. Lonfré, Mayor of Haramont.

Claude Tellier, a woodcutter, Pitou's lieutenant.

Désiré Maniquet, a poacher, Sergeant of Pitou's Company.

Bastien Godinet, one of Pitou's soldiers.

Labrie, a lackey of M. de Flesselles.

Barnaut, a stable-boy on Billot's farm.

Guyon, a turnkey in the Bastille.

Jean Bechade,
Bernard Laroche,
Jean Lacaurège,
Antoine Pujade, } prisoners in the Bastille rescued by the people.
M. de White,
Comte de Solage,
Tavernier,

LA COMTESSE DE CHARNY.

INTRODUCTORY NOTE.

"BE it understood that we are writing history, and not romance," says the author more than once in the course of these volumes. The statement is incontestable in the sense that the strictly romantic portions of the story — those which deal with fictitious personages and events — furnish but a trifling part of the interest. But, on the other hand, it must be said that he who writes of "the thing we call French Revolution" as it was, who takes its leading figures for his heroes, and describes its lurid scenes and incidents, ranging from almost incredible grandeur to quite incredible infamy and horror, — such a one, we say, could hardly fail, were he the least interesting of writers, to produce a work beside which the most intense creation of the brain of the novelist sinks into insignificance.

In "Ange Pitou" the historical thread is broken at the invasion of the *Œil-de-Bœuf* by the Parisian populace on the night of the Fifth and Sixth of October, and the fortunate, as well as courageous and tactful, interposition of Lafayette. In the "Comtesse de Charny" the narrative is resumed with the forced journey of the royal family from Versailles to Paris on the Sixth of October, and is continued, with substantial accuracy as to all the main events and innumerable minor ones, down to the Twenty-first of January, 1793, when Louis XVI., the well-meaning but fatally weak monarch, whom Carlyle calls the " unhappiest of Human Solecisms," paid the penalty of his own weakness and indecision, and the crimes and oppression of his ancestors.

Any attempt to sketch roughly these momentous years within the reasonable and proper limits of a note of this sort would necessarily result in something very like an abstract of the work to which it is introductory.

The most striking thing about this tremendous upheaval which shook the whole world, whether we read of it as told by Dumas in the various romances of the Marie Antoinette cycle, or in the numerous strictly historical works devoted to the subject, is the utter fatuity with which the king and queen — or, perhaps, the king under the influence of the queen — persistently misused, or refused to use at all, the opportunities that were afforded, in the first place to guide the Revolution, and, in the second place, when it had become too late for that, to escape by flight the consequences of their own folly.

It is a most significant fact, and one which explains much that would otherwise remain inexplicable, that previous to the flight to Varennes the French people had in but very few instances ceased to be monarchist at heart, and could very easily have been won back to the loyal support of Louis, had he chosen to adopt and consistently follow such a course of action as was promised, for instance, by his visit to the Assembly on the 4th of February, 1790, when that body was wandering in the mazes of constitution-making (whence its name "Constituent"), — had he chosen, that is to say, to accept in good faith the limited functions of kingship which that instrument allotted to him, and to be himself the leader of a peaceful revolution.

Towards the close of 1790, while disorganization and anarchy were making rapid progress, Mirabeau, "desperate of constitution-building under such accompaniments," entered into those negotiations with the court which are described with much fulness and practical accuracy by Dumas, accompanied by a marvellously truthful portrayal of him who was, beyond question, the grandest man, in everything but morals, of the whole revolutionary period. What might have been the result had he been dealt with honestly and with sincerity, it is perhaps useless to conjecture. Whether or not his ambition to save the monarchy was the offspring of his ambition to occupy the same position with respect to the queen that Mazarin is supposed to have occupied with respect to Anne of Austria, is of small consequence. It is certain that he was tricked and fooled and played with, merely to gain time, while the hope of foreign interference was growing in the queen's breast; and it is equally certain that with his death, on the 2d of April, 1791, the last chance of guiding or controlling the Revolution passed away.

And so was it with Lameth, and so, too, with Barnave, whose devotion seems to have made some impression upon Marie Antoinette, but whose only reward for his sincere purpose to serve her was premature death.

When Gamain, — of whom we believe no writer, whatever his predilections concerning the Revolution, has ever written except in terms of disgust and loathing, — when Gamain turned upon his benefactor, and disclosed the existence of the secret cupboard, the correspondence of both Barnave and Mirabeau came to light, and the evidence of their " treason " was overwhelming. Poor Barnave was then in prison as a " suspect " at Grenoble. He was brought to Paris, and guillotined in due course.

The greater statesman was beyond the reach

of the guillotine, but his remains reposed in the Panthéon, and his bust was a prominent object in the Hall of the Jacobins. The latter, denounced by Robespierre from the tribune, was cast upon the floor and shattered. But the crowning dishonor was reserved for a later period.

" It was on a dull day in autumn, in the tragical year 1794, when France had almost finished exterminating herself, — it was then that, having destroyed the living, she set about destroying the dead, and banished her most glorious son from her heart, performing this last grievous act with savage joy."

Thus Michelet, who, however, defends the action of the Convention, in pursuance of whose decree the remains of Mirabeau were removed from the Panthéon, and transported to Clamart, the burial-place for executed criminals, in the Faubourg Saint Marceau.

It may be worth while to note that the functions of friend and physician to Mirabeau, here assigned to Gilbert, were really performed by Cabanis, who published an account of his illustrious patient's last illness and death. From this contemporary source Dumas has drawn largely.

It is very difficult, after making all possible allowance for every consideration which could be humanly expected to weigh with the most exalted personages, to explain the conduct of the king and queen in connection with their attempt to join Bouillé and his army at Montmédy. They still believed, if the king may be said to have had any belief, that the Revolution might still be controlled from outside, and therefore resolved at last upon taking the step which had been urged many times by their sincere friends when secrecy would have been unnecessary. But at this time — June, 1791 — they were substantially prisoners in the Tuileries, as they had learned when they made the attempt to go to Saint Cloud in April.

Under those conditions, what steps did they take to insure secrecy, and to slip away unrecognized and unnoticed? Let us listen to Michelet on this subject: —

"This journey to Varennes was a miracle of imprudence. It is sufficient to make a statement of what common-sense required, and then to follow an opposite course; by adopting this method, if all memoirs were to vanish, the story might still be written.

"First of all, the queen orders an outfit to be made for herself and her children two or three months beforehand, as if to give notice of her departure. Next, she bespeaks a magnificent travelling-case, like the one she had already, — a complicated piece of furniture that contained all that

could have been desired for a voyage around the
globe. Then, again, instead of taking an ordinary
carriage of modest appearance, she charges Fersen
to have a huge, capacious berlin constructed, on
which might be fitted and piled a heap of trunks,
boxes, portmanteaus, and whatever else causes
a coach to be particularly conspicuous on the road.
This is not all; this coach was to be followed by
another full of female attendants; whilst before and
behind, three body-guards were to gallop as couriers
in their new bright-yellow jackets, calculated to
attract attention, and make people believe, at the
very least, that they were retainers of the Prince
de Condé, the head and front of the emigration!
Doubtless these men are familiar with the route?
No, they had never travelled it before! But they
must be resolute fellows, armed to the teeth?
They had nothing but small hunting-knives! The
king informed them that they would find arms in
the carriage; but Fersen, the queen's man, doubtless fearing on her account the danger of armed
resistance, had forgotten the weapons!

"All this is ridiculous want of foresight. But
now let us glance at the wretched, ignoble side of
the picture. The king allows himself to be dressed
as a valet, and disguises himself in a gray coat
and a little wig. He is now Durand, the *valet-de-
chambre.* These humiliating particulars are in the

simple narrative of the Duchesse d'Angoulême
(Madame Royale); the fact is also stated in the
passport given to the queen and Madame de
Tourzel, as a Russian lady, the Baroness de Korff.
Thus this lady is so intimate with her *valet-de-
chambre* (an indecorous arrangement, which alone
revealed everything) that she places him in her
carriage face to face, and knee to knee!"

And again: "A very resolute soldier, recom-
mended by M. de Bouillé, was to have entered the
carriage, to give answers when required, and to
conduct the whole affair. But Madame de Tourzel,
the governess of the royal children, insisted upon
the privilege of her office. By virtue of the oath
she had taken, it was her duty, her *right*, not to
quit the children; and the word 'oath' made a
great impression on Louis XVI. Moreover, it was
a thing unheard of in the annals of etiquette for
the Children of France to travel without a governess. Therefore the governess took her seat in the
carriage, and not the soldier; and instead of a
useful man, they had a useless woman. The expe-
dition had no leader, nobody to direct it; it was
left to go alone and at random."

In the face of these and many other similar and
indubitable facts, it is not hard to believe the anecdote of the queen's childish exploit when she en-
countered Lafayette in the Place du Carrousel.

In the details of the flight, Dumas follows Michelet very closely, assigning to the Charnys and to Billot parts which were actually played — in many instances — by unknown persons.

For example, it was not Billot, but "a scarecrow of an herb-merchant" who noticed the grand new berlin in the wood of Bondy, and furnished the needed information as to the road the fugitives had taken. So Drouet, when he rode out of Sainte Menehould, was "watched and closely followed by a horseman who understood his intention, and would, perhaps, have killed him; but he galloped across the country and plunged into the woods, where it was impossible to overtake him." And Romœuf arrived at Varennes from Paris, accompanied by "an officer of the National Guard, — a man of gloomy countenance, evidently fatigued, but agitated and excited, wearing plain, unpowdered hair, and a shirt open at the neck."

It was Count Fersen, a Swede, who drove the berlin to Bondy. He seems to have been influenced solely by attachment to the queen. He disappears from history from the time he left the coach at Bondy.

The three body-guards who accompanied the flight were Valory, Malden, and Du Moustier. They were gagged, and bound upon the seat of the carriage on the return to Paris.

Madame Campan, the queen's *femme-de-chambre*, is authority for many details given by Dumas, — as, for instance, the secrecy observed by Marie Antoinette in her interviews with Barnave, and as to the precautions adopted with respect to food, having their source in the return to the Tuileries of the Palais-Royal pastry-cook, who was such a furious Jacobin.

Madame Campan also testifies to the enormous appetite of the king, and to the queen's mortification because it never abated; nor did he put any restraint upon it, no matter how painful or humiliating were his circumstances.

The League of Pilnitz, in August, 1791, made the king's eventual deposition inevitable, although it was postponed for a year. The manifesto issued by the parties to the league aroused furious indignation in France. The flames which it kindled were not extinguished till twenty-five years later.

In September, the Constituent Assembly, having previously, upon Robespierre's motion, declared its members ineligible for the succeeding Assembly, declared its sessions to be ended, and went its way.

On October 1, the Legislative Assembly, the first and last body elected under the Constitution, began its life of a year.

Its time was wasted in " debates, futilities, and staggering parliamentary procedure," amid frequent changes of ministry, growing anxiety concerning foreign invasion, and such internal episodes as that of Avignon, where the reprisals for the death of L'Escuyer, under the lead of Jourdan Coupe-Tête, were immeasurably worse than is here hinted at. The Tour de la Glacière was the theatre of scenes at the mere thought of which the heart sickens.

In those chapters of the "Comtesse de Charny" which deal with the ministry of Dumouriez, and the events accompanying and succeeding it, we have some welcome glimpses of "that queen-like burgher-woman, beautiful Amazonian — graceful to the eye ; more so to the mind," — the daughter of Phlipon, the Paris engraver, and wife of Roland de la Platrière. " The creature of sincerity and nature " — so she has been described — " in an age of artificiality, pollution, and cant ; there, in her still completeness, in her. still invincibility, *she*, if thou knew it, is the noblest of all living Frenchwomen."

In due time the Girondist deputies, to the number of some twenty or more, succumbed to the Mountain, and ascended the fatal platform, from which they might have saved Louis XVI., had they had the courage to vote in accordance with their acknowledged convictions.

On the 8th of November, 1793, a month after the death of the queen, and within a day or two of the last appearance upon earth of Madame Du Barry,

who has been called the "gateway of the Revolu-
tion," and the infamous Philippe Égalité, Madame
Roland followed her associates to the Place de la
Révolution.

Her memoirs were written during the five months
she was in prison.

Events marched fast during the early summer
of 1792, following the declaration of war against
Austria in April. The Clubs, journalistic organiza-
tions, and Sections were growing ever more violent
and desperate, and on June 20th came the immense
procession, which eventually invaded the Tuileries,
— an occasion more remarkable for what it fore-
boded than for what actually happened.

Lafayette's unexpected appearance in the Assembly a week later put the finishing touch to the
extinction of his popularity and influence upon
events.

The scene in the Assembly on July 6th, deri-
sively called the " Baiser l'amourette," was followed
by Barbaroux's famous despatch to Rebecqui for
" five hundred men who know how to die."

The solemn proclamation of the " Country in
Danger " on July 22d, the Prussian declaration of
war on the 24th, and the celebrated, but ill-advised,
manifesto of the Duke of Brunswick carried the
excitement and indignation of France to the boiling
point. The arrival at Paris of the black-browed

Marseillais, after "wending their wild way from the extremity of French land, through unknown cities, toward unknown destiny, with a purpose that they know," inspired to frenzy by the soul-stirring strains of the "Marseillaise," the "luckiest musical composition ever promulgated," — their arrival at Paris, we say, in the last days of July, furnished the only ingredient that was lacking to make the seething mass of the population effervesce, and the Tenth of August was the inevitable sequel.

Of all the participants in the events of that dreadful day, the interest of humanity must ever attach most compassionately to the devoted Swiss. The ten score or more of courtiers who had rushed to the Tuileries to defend monarchy in its last ditch succeeded in escaping in large numbers when they found themselves shamelessly deserted by those for whom they had come to lay down their lives. Some there were who remained and faced certain death heroically; but they were Frenchmen dying for what they thought a consecrated cause. How different was it with the Swiss! They were mere "hirelings," as they had been often sneeringly called; by birth and education, their sympathies were on the popular side; they had no interest in maintaining their position, except to obey the order of him to whom they had sold their services, and by him they had been heartlessly abandoned. They knew not how to act: "one duty only is clear to them, that of standing by their post; and they will perform that."

Westermann pleaded with them in German, and the Marseillais implored them " in hot Provençal speech and pantomime." Let them stand aside, and their lives were saved. They stood fast, and what followed is known of all men.

The consequences of the Tenth of August were not slow to follow, as the Assembly in the presence of the king voted that the " Hereditary Representative " (which was the constitutional title of the king) be suspended. It also voted that a NATIONAL CONVENTION be summoned, by election, to provide for the future.

Meanwhile, and until that Convention assembled, although the Legislature continued to sit, the Insurrectionary Commune, self-constituted, was really supreme at Paris, and Danton held the seals of the Department of Justice.

The removal of the royal family to the Temple, and their life there, are told by Dumas in much detail and with complete fidelity to history, which necessarily relies for many of its facts upon the narratives of the *valets-de-chambre*.

We need add nothing either to what our author has to say with relation to the " Massacres of Sep-

tember" at La Force and the other prisons, except
that the massacred amounted to one thousand and
eighty-nine, all told, and that Robespierre "nearly
wept" at the thought that one innocent person was
slain! It is said that the bell of Saint-Germain
l'Auxerrois, on which the tocsin was sounded for the
massacres to begin, was the identical metal on which
the signal was given for the Saint Bartholomew, two
hundred and twenty years before.

Twenty-three theatres were open while the
slaughter was in progress!

Both Sombreuil and Cazotte were spared, at the
intercession of their daughters, but both subsequently came to the guillotine during the "Terror."

Maillard's appearance as presiding officer of the
tribunal at La Force was his last in history.

The most important incidents of the famous sitting of the Convention at which the death of Louis
was decreed, mainly through the weakness of
Vergniaud and his fellow Girondists, are described
by Dumas in accordance with all the authorities,
and the same may be said of his description of the
king's last hours and execution.

The author's frequent eulogistic references to
Michelet, whom, as we have said, he follows closely
in many portions of the narrative, make it proper
to say that the impartiality of that writer is by no
means beyond question. In a note to one of the

earlier romances of this series, we have adverted to the charge he has brought against Louis XV. apparently without authority, and that charge is echoed by Dumas in these volumes almost every time that Comte Louis de Narbonne is mentioned.

It is natural that so earnest a partisan of the Revolution should be influenced by bitter feelings towards England for the part she played under the leadership of Pitt and Burke. But it can hardly be claimed that he is justified in characterizing Burke as "a talented, but passionate and venal Irishman," who "was paid by his adversary, Mr. Pitt," for "a furious philippic against the Revolution;" or in speaking of that statesman's work as "an infamous book, wild with rage, full of calumny, scurrilous abuse, and insulting buffoonery;" or, again, in referring to him as a man "possessed of brilliant eloquence, but devoid of ideas and of frivolous character," — a man "who makes the better actor because he acts his part in earnest, and because his interior emptiness enables him the better to adopt and urge the ideas of others;" or in making the statement that "England never had, nor will she ever have, any great moralist or jurisconsult."

Olivier de Charny is a most perfect type of many noble-hearted Frenchmen who sacrificed their lives without a murmur in behalf of what they believed to be a holy cause, convinced though they were of the comparative unworthiness of those who stood for that cause. It was fitting that Andrée, whose only happiness in life had come to her through him, and whose hopes of happiness died with him, should have turned aside from the thought of life without him.

In view of the terrible months that followed the death of the king, happy were they who, like Gilbert and Billot, turned their backs upon their country, and sought true freedom under the flag of the new Republic across the sea.

In the last volume of the series, " Chevalier de Maison Rouge," the author has taken for his theme the agony of Marie Antoinette during the eight months that intervened between the king's death and her own. We shall there make the acquaintance of one whose devotion was to the person of the queen even more than to the dying cause which she represented.

LA COMTESSE DE CHARNY.

LIST OF CHARACTERS.

Period, 1789–1794.

LOUIS XVI., King of France.

MARIE ANTOINETTE.

THE DAUPHIN,
MADAME ROYALE, } the royal children.

MADAME ELIZABETH, the King's sister.

COMTE DE PROVENCE,
COMTE D'ARTOIS, } brothers of the King.

PRINCESSE DE LAMBALLE, Superintendent of the royal household.

M. DE PENTHIÈVRE, her father-in-law.

MADAME DE TOURZEL, governess of the royal children.

MADAME MISERY,
MADAME CAMPAN, } the Queen's waiting-women.
MADAME NEUVILLE,

WEBER, confidential servant to Marie Antoinette.

DOCTOR LOUIS, Marie Antoinette's physician.

MADAME BRUNIER, the Dauphin's chambermaid.

M. DE BRÉZÉ, Master of Ceremonies.

LA CHAPELLE, the King's steward.

MM. HUE, DAREY, and THIERRY, attendants of the King.

PRINCE DE POIX,
M. DE SAINT-PARDON,
BARON D'AUBIER,
MM. DE GOGUELAT and DE CHAMILLÉ,
} gentlemen of the King's household after the 10th of August.

CLÉRY, the King's valet at the Temple.

M. LÉONARD, the Queen's hairdresser.

ROYALISTS.

PRINCE DE CONDÉ.	MARQUIS DE FAVRAS.
DUC DE LIANCOURT.	BARON DE BRETEUIL.
DUC DE LA ROCHEFOUCAULT.	DUC DE MAILLY.
COMTE DE LA MARCK.	MARÉCHAL DE MOUCHY.
COMTESSE DE LA MARCK.	MARÉCHAL DE NOAILLES.
COMTE LOUIS DE NARBONNE.	DUC DE CASTRIES.
COMTE FERSEN.	COMTE D'INNISDAL.
BARONESS DE STAËL.	DUC CHARLES DE LORRAINE
PRINCE DE LAMBESQ.	ABBÉ SICARD.

MM. VIOMESNIL, DE LA CHÂTRE, LECROSNE, GOSSE, VILLIERS,
    and BRIDAUD.

M. DE DAMPIERRE, Chevalier of the Order of Saint Louis.

PIERRE VICTOR BESENVAL, Inspector-General of Swiss.

M. LAPORTE, Superintendent of the Civil List.

M. DE VILLEROY, of the King's household.

M. PASTORET, a member of the Legislative Assembly.

M. DE BRISSAC, Commander of the King's Constitutional Guard.

M. DE SOMBREUIL, Governor of Hôtel des Invalides.

MADEMOISELLE DE SOMBREUIL, his daughter.

M. ACLOQUE, a Commander of the National Guard.

MM. DE CARTEJA, CLERMONT, D'AMBOISE, TOURCATY, D'AMBLAY,
    MARQUIÉ, and MERCI D'ARGENTEAU.

PRINCESSE DE LA TRÉMOUILLE.	BARON DE BATZ.
MADAME DE MACKAU.	PARISOT, a journalist.
MADAME DE LA ROCHE AYMON.	JACQUES CAZOTTE.
MADAME GINESTOUS.	MADEMOISELLE CAZOTTE, his
PRINCESSE DE TARENTE.	daughter.

M. DE MALDEN,
M. DE VALORY, } accompanying the royal family
COMTE OLIVIER DE CHARNY, } in the flight from Paris.

COMTESSE DE CHARNY, the Queen's maid-of-honor.

VICOMTE ISIDORE DE CHARNY, Comte de Charny's brother.

ROYALISTS.

ABBÉ BOUYON, a dramatic author,
M. DE SULEAU, a Royalist pamphleteer,   } killed by the mob of
MM. VIGIER and SOLMINIAC, of the   August 10th.
old Royal Guard,

M. DE MONTMORIN,
ABBÉ DE RASTIGNAC, a religious author,   } victims of the Sep-
ABBÉ LENFANT, an ex-chaplain of the King,   tember massacre.

Royalist Officers assisting in the Flight of the Royal Family.

MARQUIS DE BOUILLÉ, Governor-General of the City of Metz.
COMTE LOUIS DE BOUILLÉ,   } his sons.
M. JULES DE BOUILLÉ,

DUC DE CHOISEUL.   MARQUIS DE DANDOINS.
BARON DE MANDELL.   COLONEL DE DAMAS.
LIEUTENANT BONDET.   CAPTAIN DESLON.
ADJUTANT FOCQ.   CAPTAIN GUNTZER.
SERGEANT SAINT CHARLES.   SERGEANT LA POTTERIE.
MM. DE FLOIRAC, ROHRIG, and RAIGECOURT.

Royalist Officers defending the Tuileries.

M. D'HERVILLY, commanding the Chevaliers of Saint Louis and
Constitutional Guard.
GENERAL MANDAT, a Commander of the National Guard.
M. MAILLARDOT, commanding the Swiss.
M. DE CHANTEREINE, Colonel of the King's Constitutional
Guard.
CHEVALIER CHARLES D'AUTICHAMP.
SALIS LIZERS, MAJOR READING, and CAPTAIN DURLER, Swiss
officers.
MM. RULHIÈRES, VERDIÈRE, DE LA CHESNAYE, and FORESTIER
DE SAINT-VENANT.

202 LISTLIST OF CHARACTERS.

REVOLUTIONISTS.REVOLUTIONISTS.

JEAN PAUL MARAT, editor of " L'Ami du Peuple."

MAXIMILIEN DE ROBESPIERRE, an advocate of Arras, member
of the National Assembly and of the National Convention.

DANTON, Minister of Justice and Member of the National
Convention.

LOUIS PHILIPPE JOSEPH, DUC D'ORLÉANS, afterwards called
Philippe Égalité.

ROUGET DE L'ISLE, an engineering officer of Strasburg, author
of " La Marseillaise."

SANTERRE, a brewer, General-in-Chief of a Battalion of the
National Guard.

GONCHON, " the Mirabeau of the People."

FOUQUIER TINVILLE, Attorney-General of the Revolutionary
Tribunal.

ANTOINE SAINT JUST,
BILLAUD DE VARENNES,
HÉRAULT DE SÉCHELLES,
COLLET D'HERBOIS,
LEGENDRE, a butcher,   members of the National
ANACHARSIS CLOOTZ,   Convention condemning
THURIOT, called " the king-killer,"   the King.
COUTHON, a cripple,
FABRE D'EGLANTINE,
LEPELLETIER DE SAINT FARGEAU,
BISHOP GRÉGOIRE,

MAILLARD, Sheriff of the Court of the Châtelet.

THÉROIGNE DU MÉRICOURT, a courtesan.

THOMAS PAINE.   DUC D'AIGUILLON.

M. ROBERT.   FOURNIER, an American.

WESTERMANN, a Prussian.

NICHOLAS, a butcher.

PROSPER VERRIÈRES, a deformed dwarf.

HENRIOT, the master of the guillotine.

REVOLUTIONISTS.

SIMON, a cobbler, in charge of the Dauphin at the Temple.

MESSIEURS ISABEY, father and son.

MADAME DE ROCHEREUL, a spy at the Tuileries.

CHABOT, one of the authors of the "Catechism for Sans Culottes."

LACROIX, a lawyer, member of the Legislative Assembly.

BISHOP TORNÉ, of the Legislative Assembly.

ANDRÉ CHÉNIER, a poet.

BERTRAND BARRÈRE, member of the National Convention.

COUNT D'OYAT, a bastard son of Louis XV.

VIRCHAUX, a Swiss.   BRUSNE, a type-setter.

BONJOUR, a clerk in the Navy Department.

MADAME CANDEILLE, of the Comédie Française, actress, poetess, musician.

NICHOLAS CLAUDE GAMAIN, master locksmith to the King.

MATTHEW JOUVE, otherwise known as Jourdan the headsman.
MM. LESCUYER, DUPRAT, and MAINVIELLE, } Avignon Revolutionists.

CHARLOT, a barber,
GRISON, RODI, and MAMIN, } murderers of Princesse de Lamballe.

M. HUGUENIN, President of the Commune.

M. TALLIEN, Secretary of the Commune.

MM. MANUEL and CHAUMETTE, Procureurs of the Commune.

LUZOUSKI, a Pole, member of the Communal Council.

PANIS, friend of Danton and brother-in-law of Santerre,
MM. JORDEUIL and DUPLAIN,
SERGENT, a copper-plate engraver, } of the Communal Council and Vigilance Committee.

MM. DEFORGUES, GUERMER, DUFORT, LENFANT, and LECLERC, of the Vigilance Committee.

CAMBON, Guardian of the Public Treasures.

MOUCHET, a crippled dwarf, Justice of the Peace from the Marais District.

REVOLUTIONISTS.

LUBIN, a municipal officer proclaiming the Republic.

BOUCHER RENÉ,
BOUCHER SAINT-SAUVEUR, } municipal officials.
MM. BOIRIE and LE ROULX,

M. GIRAUD, City Architect of Paris.

REVOLUTIONARY JOURNALISTS.

CAMILLE DESMOULINS, styling himself "Procureur-Général de la Lanterne."

JACQUES RENÉ HÉBERT, editor of Father Duchêne.

LOUIS STANISLAUS FRÉRON, editor of "Le Moniteur."

LOUSTALOT,
CITIZEN PROUDHOMME, } editors of "Révolutions de Paris."

M. CARRA, editor of "Annales Patriotiques."

BONNEVILLE, editor of "The Iron Mouth."

JEAN LAMBERT TALLIEN, editor of "L'Ami des Citoyens."

MADEMOISELLE DE KÉRALIO, writer for the "Mercury," afterwards Madame Robert.

GIRONDISTS.

JEANNE MARIE ROLAND DE LA PLATIÈRE.

MANON JEANNE PHLIPON, his wife, usually called Madame Roland.

CHARLES BARBAROUX, of Marseilles,
M. REBECQUI, his friend,
M. GRANGENEUVE, a Bordeaux advocate,
JEANNE PIERRE BRISSOT,
JEROME PÉTION,
RABAUT SAINT-ÉTIENNE,
GIREY DUPRÉ,
ABBÉ FAUCHET,
MM. LOUVET, ISNARD, BOYER FONFRÈDE,
CONDORCET, VERGNIAUD, GENSONNÉ,
GUADET, LANJUINAIS, VALAZÉ,
LASOURCE, BIROTTEAU, DUCOS,
DUCHÂTEL,
} members of the National Convention.

M. BAILLY, an astronomer, Provost of the
    Merchants of Paris,

PIERRE JOSEPH MARIE DE BARNAVE,

ADRIEN DUPORT,

> members of the National Assembly, — leaders of the Constitutional Party.

M. LA HARPE, author of " Mélanie,"

M. ANDRIEUX, an author.

M. SEDAINE, a gem-cutter,

CHAMFORT, poet-laureate,

MARIE-JOSEPH CHÉNIER, author of " Charles IX."

M. LACLOS, author of " Les Liaisons Dangereuses,"

LAÏS, a singer,

NAPOLEON BONAPARTE, a Lieutenant of Artillery,

TALMA, LARIVE, } actors,   DAVID, VERNET, } painters,

MM. BARRAS, CHODIEU, CHAPELLIER, and MONT-LOSIER,

> members of the Jacobin Club.

HONORÉ GABRIEL VICTOR RIQUETTI, COMTE DE
    MIRABEAU,

DOCTOR GUILLOTIN, inventor of the guillotine,

CHARLES DE LAMETH,

ALEXANDRE DE BEAUHARNAIS,

ABBÉS DE SIÈYES and MAURY,

PRIEUR DE LA MARNE,

REGNAULT DE SAINT JEAN D'ANGÉLY,

MM. THOURET, SALLES, MOUNIER, BUZOT, LALLY,
    DESMEUNIERS, GUILHERMY, MALHOUET, TAR-
    GET, and DE LATOUR MAUBOURG,

> of the National Assembly.

MARQUIS DE LAFAYETTE, Commander-in-Chief of the National
    Guard,

MARQUIS DE CHATEAUNEUF,

FRANÇOIS DE NEUFCHATEAU,

CAMUS, the Recorder,

MM. COCHON, GRANDPRÉ, ROUYER,
    LEQUINIO, and QUINETTE,

> members of the National Convention.

BARON DE NECKER, Prime Minister, 1789–90.

CHEVALIER DE GRAVE,
M. CAHIER DE GERVILLE, } of the King's Council in 1792.

GENERAL DUMOURIEZ, Secretary of Foreign Affairs in 1792.

M. LACOSTE, Minister of the Navy,
M. CLAVIÈRES, Minister of Finance,
M. DURANTHON, Minister of Justice,
M. SERVAN, Secretary of War (Chevalier de Grave's successor), } of the Dumouriez Ministry.

M. CHAMBONNAS, Secretary of Foreign Affairs, succeeding General Dumouriez.

M. LAJARD, Secretary of War, his colleague.

M. MONGE, Minister of the Navy under the Republic.

M. DE NOAILLES, French Ambassador at Vienna.

M. DE SÉGUR, Ambassador at Berlin.

MARÉCHAL DE ROCHAMBEAU,
GENERALS LUCKNER, KELLERMAN, BEAUREPAIRE, CUSTINE, BEURNONVILLE, and CHAZOT,
LIEUTENANT-COLONEL BERTOIS,
THEOBALD DILLON,
MM. DE BIRON and DE WATTEVILLE, } officers of the French armies on the frontiers.

MATHAY, keeper of the Temple Tower.

TURGY, an attendant of the Princesses at the Temple.

TISON,
MADAME TISON, } municipal spies at the Temple.

CITIZENS GOBEAU, DANJOU, JACQUES ROUX, TURLOT, and MEUNIER,
JAMES, a teacher of English, } municipal officials on duty at the Temple.

ROCHER, a janitor at the Temple.

MM. MALESHERBES, TRONCHET, and DESÈZE, advocates defending the King.

M. GARAT, Minister of Justice,
M. LEBRUN, Minister of Foreign Affairs,
M. GROVELLE, Secretary of the Council, } members of the Executive Council notifying the King of his sentence.

ABBÉ EDGEWORTH DE FIRMONT, the King's confessor at his execution.

CITIZEN RICAVE, rector of Saint Madeleine, ⎫

CITIZENS RENARD and DAMOREAU, vicars ⎪ making the official

of Saint Madeleine Parish, ⎬ report of the in-

CITIZENS LEBLANC and DUBOIS, Adminis- ⎪ terment of the

trators of the Department of Paris, ⎭ King.

COMTE CAGLIOSTRO, assuming the name of Baron Zannone, a Genoese banker.

DOCTOR HONORÉ GILBERT, physician to the King.

SEBASTIEN GILBERT, his son.

JEAN BAPTISTE TOUSSAINT DE BEAUSIRE, an adventurer.

NICOLE OLIVA LEGAY, "a woman resembling the Queen."

TOUSSAINT, son of Beausire and Nicole.

ARCHBISHOP OF BORDEAUX, BISHOP OF AUTUN.

THE CURATES OF SAINT PAUL'S and AGENTEUIL.

MM. DE ROMEUF and GOUVIN, aides-de-camp to Lafayette.

ROMAINVILLIERS, a commander of the National Guard.

MATTHEW DUMAS, an aide-de-camp in the National Guard.

FARMER-GENERAL AUGEAUD.

MARCEAU, a member of the City Council.

PROCUREUR-SYNDIC ROEDERER.

CHARLES LOUIS SANSON, commonly called Monsieur de Paris.

CITIZEN PALLOY, municipal architect.

MADAME VILLETTE, Voltaire's adopted daughter.

MADEMOISELLE CHARLOTTE DE ROBESPIERRE, sister of Robespierre.

MADAME D'ARAZON, Mirabeau's niece.

MADAME DU SAILLANT, Mirabeau's sister.

ALBERTINE, wife of Marat.

MADAME DANTON.

LUCILE DUPLESSIS LARIDON, wife of Camille Desmoulins.

MM. DUMONT and FRICHOT, friends of Mirabeau.

CÉRUTTI, pronouncing the eulogy at Mirabeau's funeral.

DOCTOR CABANIS.

M. Lescuyer, a notary at Avignon.

Major Préfontaine.

Jean Baptiste Drouet, son of the post-superintendent at St. Menehould.

Gillaume,
Maugin, } assisting Drouet to arrest the King's flight.

M. Sausse, town solicitor of Varennes.

Madame Sausse.

Hannont, commander of the National Guard of Varennes.

Dietrich, Mayor of Strasburg.

M. Champagneux, editor of " The Lyons Journal."

MM. Bosc, Bancal des Issarts, and Lanthenas, friends of Monsieur and Madame Roland.

M. Sourdat, a lawyer of Troyes, offering to defend the King.

Ogé, a Saint Domingo negro.

Madame Dugazon, a singer.

Saint-Prix, an actor.

Olympe de Gouges, a dramatic writer.

Caron de Beaumarchais, author of " Figaro."

Fleur d'Épine, a recruiting officer.

Father Rémy, a military pensioner.

Pelline, Mirabeau's secretary.

Teisch and Jean, Mirabeau's servants.

Fritz, Count Cagliostro's servant.

Mallet, a wine dealer.

Duplay, a joiner.

Madame Duplay, his wife.

Mademoiselle Duplay.

Baptiste, servant of Comte de Charny.

Leclerc, an amorer.

Master Guidon, a carpenter.

Brisack, servant of M. de Choiseul.

Hucher and François, bakers.

Buseby, a wig-maker.

Lajariette, a barber.

The Register of the Court of the Châtelet.
Louis, a turnkey at the Châtelet prison.
Frederick William, King of Prussia.
The Duke of Brunswick.
Countess Lichtenau.
Comte Clerfayt, an Austrian General.
William Pitt, the Younger.

RESIDENTS OF VILLERS COTTERETS.

Billot, a farmer, afterwards a Deputy to the Legislative
   Assembly, condemning the King.
Catherine, his daughter.
Isidore, son of Catherine and Vicomte de Charny.
Madame Billot.
M. de Longpré, Mayor of Villers Cotteret.
Abbé Fortier.
Mademoiselle Adelaide, his niece.
Ange Pitou, Captain of the National Guard of Haramont.
Désiré Maniquet, Pitou's lieutenant.
Claude Tellier, Sergeant of the Haramont National Guard.
Messieurs Boulanger and Molicar, of Pitou's troops.
Doctor Raynal.
Madame Clément, a nurse.
Father Clouis.
Father Lajeunesse.
Master Delauroy, } tailors.
Master Bligny,
Picard, a locksmith.
Mother Colombe, distributor of letters.
Mother Fagot.
Fagotin, her son.
Farolet.
Rigolet, a locksmith.

THE

CHEVALIER DE MAISON-ROUGE.

INTRODUCTORY NOTE.

The "Chevalier de Maison-Rouge," though it
deals with events subsequent to those covered by
the earlier stories of the Marie Antoinette cycle,
was written at an earlier date. In it we are introduced to a new set of personages, and see no more
of the characters whose fortunes furnish the fictitious as distinguished from the historical interest of
the earlier stories.

The months which elapsed between the execution
of the King and the appearance in the Place de la
Révolution of the ill-fated Marie Antoinette were
thickly strewn with tragedy, particularly after the
final conflict between the Gironde and the Mountain, and the decisive victory of the latter, resulting
in the undisputed supremacy of the band of men
in whom we now see the personification of the Reign
of Terror.

Those portions of the narrative which describe
the life of the queen at the Temple, and subse-

quently in the Conciergerie, are founded strictly
upon fact. Of the treatment accorded to the little
Dauphin by Simon, who is given much prominence
in the story, it need only be said that it falls far
short of the truth as it is to be found in number-
less memoirs and documents. There is nothing in
all history more touching and heartrending than the
fate of this innocent child, who was literally done to
death by sheer brutality in less than two years;
nor is there any one of the excesses committed by
the extreme revolutionists which has done more to
cause posterity to fail to realize the vast benefits
which mankind owes to the Revolution, in the face
of the unnamable horrors which were perpetrated
in its name.

The noble answer of Marie Antoinette to the
unnatural charges brought against her by Hébert
(not Simon) was actually made at her trial.

There is no direct historical authority for the
various attempts herein detailed to effect the escape
of the Queen, although rumors of such were circu-
lating unceasingly. The titular hero of the book
is not an historical personage, nor are Maurice
Lindey and Lorin; but the latter are faithful representatives of a by no means small class of
sincere and devoted republicans who turned aside

with shrinking horror from the atrocities of the Terror.

The mutual heroism of Maurice and Lorin in the final catastrophe reminds us of the similar conduct of Gaston in the "Regent's Daughter" when he fails to reach Nantes with the reprieve until the head of one of his comrades had fallen. Nor can one avoid a thought of Sydney Carton laying down his life for Charles Darnay, in Charles Dickens's "Tale of Two Cities," wherein the horrors of the Terror are so vividly pictured.

One must go far to seek for a more touching and pathetic love-episode than that of Maurice and Geneviève, whose sinning, if sinning it was, was forced upon them by the cold and unscrupulous Dixmer in the pursuit of his one unchangeable idea.

On the 16th of October, 1793, the daughter of the Cæsars lost her life through the instrumentality of the machine which we saw Cagliostro exhibit to her in a glass of water at the Château de Taverney more than twenty years before. Then she was in the bloom of youth and beauty, a young queen coming to reign over a people who had just begun to realize their wrongs and their power. To-day she is a woman of thirty-eight, prema-

turely aged, but bearing about her still the noble
dignity of her ancient race, and proving anew, as
Charles I. had proved, and as her own husband
had proved, that the near approach of death
brings forth the noblest qualities in those of royal
lineage.

We cannot better end this brief note than by
quoting the characteristic but powerful apostrophe
of Carlyle in his essay upon the "Diamond
Necklace."

"Beautiful Highborn, thou wert so foully hurled
low! For if thy being came to thee out of old
Hapsburg dynasties, came it not also (like my own)
out of Heaven? *Sunt lachrymæ rerum, et mentem
mortalia tangunt.* Oh, is there a man's heart that
thinks without pity of those long months and years
of slow-wasting ignominy: of thy birth, soft-cradled
in imperial Schönbrunn, the winds of Heaven not
to visit thy face too roughly, thy foot to light on
softness, thy eye on splendor: and then of thy
death, or hundred deaths, to which the guillotine
and Fouquier-Tinville's judgment bar was but the
merciful end? Look *there*, O man born of woman!
The bloom of that fair face is wasted, the hair
is gray with care: the brightness of those eyes is
quenched, their lids hang drooping, the face is

stony pale, as of one living in death. Mean weeds,
which her own hand has mended, attire the Queen
of the World. The death-hurdle, where thou sittest
pale, motionless, which only curses environ, has to
stop; a people, drunk with vengeance, will drink it
again in full draught, looking at thee there. Far
as the eye reaches, a multitudinous sea of maniac
heads: the air deaf with their triumph yell! The
living-dead must shudder with yet one other pang:
her startled blood yet again suffuses with the hue
of agony that pale face which she hides with her
hands. There is, then, no heart to say, God pity
thee? O think not of these: think of HIM whom
thou worshippest, the Crucified, — who also treading
the wine-press *alone*, fronted sorrow still deeper:
and triumphed over it, and made it holy: and built
of it a Sanctuary of Sorrow for thee and all the
wretched! Thy path of thorns is nigh ended.
One long last look at the Tuileries, where thy step
was once so light, — where thy children shall not
dwell. The head is on the block: the axe rushes —
Dumb lies the World: that wild-yelling World and
all its madness is behind thee."

CHEVALIER DE MAISON-ROUGE.

LIST OF CHARACTERS.

Period, 1793.

Marie Antoinette,
The Dauphin,
Madame Royale,
The Princess Elizabeth,
} prisoners at the Temple.

Chevalier de Maison-Rouge,
M. Dixmer,
Geneviève, his wife,
Sophie Tison,
} engaged in an attempt to rescue the Queen.

Lieutenant Maurice Lindey, a patriot, in love with Geneviève.
Maximilien-Jean Lorin, his friend.
Santerre, Commandant of the Parisian National Guard.
Simon, a cobbler.
President Harmand, of the Revolutionary Tribunal.
Fouquier-Tinville, the public accuser.
M. Giraud, the city architect.
Chauveau Lagarde, counsel for the Queen.

Jean Paul Marot,
Robespierre,
Danton,
Chénier,
Hébert,
Fabre d'Églantine,
Collot d'Herbois,
Robert Lindet,
} Montagnards.

MM. Vergniaud, Feraud, Brissot, Louvet, } Girondins.
    Pétion, Valazé, Lanjuinais, Barbaroux, }

MM. Roland, Servien, Clavières, } of the French Ministry,
    Le Brun, and Monge, }   August, 1793.

Generals Dumouriez, Miacrinski, } officers commanding the
    Steingel, Neuilly, Valence, } French armies on the
    Dampierre, and Miranda, }   frontiers.

Henriot, Commandant-General of the National Guard.

Citizen Devaux, of the National Guard.

Citizens Tonlan, Lepitre, Agricola, } of the Municipal
    and Mercevault, }   Guard.

Grammont, Adjutant-Major.

Tison, employed at the Temple Prison.

Madame Tison, his wife.

Arthémise, ex-dancer at the opera.

Abbé Girard.

Dame Jacinthe, his servant.

Turgy, an old waiter of Louis XVI., attending the royal family at the Temple.

Muguet, *femme-de-chambre* of Dixmer.

Madame Plumeau, hostess of an alehouse near the Temple.

Agesilaus, servant to Maurice Lindey.

Aristide, concierge at Maurice's house.

Gracchus, a turnkey at the Conciergerie.

Richard, jailer at the Conciergerie.

Madame Richard, his wife.

Duchesse, } Gendarmes at the Conciergerie.
Gilbert, }

Sanson, the executioner.

THE COUNT OF MONTE CRISTO.

LIST OF CHARACTERS.

Period, 1815-1838.

EDMOND DANTÈS, a Marseilles sailor, mate of the " Pharaon," afterwards Count of Monte Cristo, assuming the names of Lord Wilmore, Abbé Busoni, and Sinbad the Sailor.

LOUIS DANTÈS, his father.

MERCÉDÈS, a catalan, betrothed to Edmond Dantès.

FERNAND MONDEGO, her cousin, afterwards Comte de Morcerf.

VICOMTE ALBERT DE MORCERF, his son.

DANGLARS, supercargo of the " Pharaon," afterwards Baron Danglars, a Paris banker.

BARONNE DANGLARS, his wife.

MADEMOISELLE EUGÈNIE DANGLARS, their daughter.

LOUISE D'ARMILLY, her music-teacher and friend.

M. MORELL, owner of the " Pharaon."

MADAME MORELL.

MAXIMILIAN MORELL,
JULIE MORELL,
} their children.

EMMANUEL HERBAUT,
COCLÈS,
} clerks in the house of Morell and Sons, Marseilles.

GASPARD CADEROUSSE, a Marseilles tailor, afterwards landlord of the Pont du Gard Inn.

MADELEINE, his wife, otherwise known as La Carconte.

THE EMPEROR NAPOLEON.

LOUIS XVIII.

BARON DANDRÉ, Minister of Police, } Royalists.
DUC DE BLACAS,

M. NOIRTIER DE VILLEFORT, an adherent of Napoleon.

M. GÉRARD DE VILLEFORT, his son, *procureur du roi*.

MARQUIS DE SAINT-MÉRAN.

MARQUISE DE SAINT-MÉRAN.

MADEMOISELLE RENÉE DE SAINT-MÉRAN, their daughter, betrothed to M. Gérard de Villefort.

COMTE DE SALVIEUX, friend of M. de Saint-Méran.

GENERAL FLAVIEN DE QUESNEL.

BARON FRANZ D'ÉPINAY, his son.

LIEUTENANT-COLONEL LOUIS JACQUES BEAUREPAIRE, } members of the Bonapartist Club in the Rue St. Jacques.
BRIGADIER-GENERAL ÉTIENNE DUCHAMPY,
CLAUDE LECHARPAL, keeper of streams and forests,

MARÉCHEL BERTRAND.

M. DE BOVILLE, inspector of prisons.

THE GOVERNOR OF THE CHÂTEAU D'IF.

ABBÉ FARIA, a prisoner in the Château d'If.

A JAILOR, at the Château d'If.

THE MAYOR OF MARSEILLES.

CAPTAIN BALDI, of "La Jeune Amélie," a Genoese smuggler.

JACOPO, one of his crew.

MAÎTRE PASTRINI, proprietor of the Hôtel de Londres, Rome.

GAETANO, a Roman sailor.

CUCUMETTO, a brigand chief.

CARLINI, } of Cucumetto's troop.
DIAVOLACCIO,

RITA, betrothed to Carlini.

LUIGI VAMPA, a shepherd boy, afterwards a Captain of Roman brigands.

TERESA, his betrothed.

PEPPINO, a shepherd.

ANDREA RONDOLA, a condemned murderer.

COMTE DE SAN FELICE, } Roman noblemen.
DUC DE BRACCIANO, }

CARMELA, Comte de San Felice's daughter.

COMTESSE GUICCIOLI.

MAJOR BARTOLOMEO CAVALCANTI, an adventurer.

BENEDETTO, passing under the name of Andrea de Cavalcanti.

M. LUCIEN DEBRAY, private secretary }
    to the Minister of the Interior, } friends of Albert de
M. BEAUCHAMP, an editor, } Morcerf.
COMTE DE CHÂTEAU-RENAUD, }

HÉLOÏSE, Villefort's second wife.

ÉDOUARD, her son.

MADEMOISELLE VALENTINE, Villefort's daughter by his first
    wife, in love with Maximilian Morell.

DOCTOR D'AVRIGNY, Villefort's physician.

M. DESCHAMPS, a notary.

ALI TEBELIN, Pacha of Janina.

VASILIKI, his wife.

HAYDÉE, daughter of Ali Pacha and Vasiliki.

SELIM, favorite of Ali Pacha.

BERTUCCIO, steward to the Count of Monte Cristo.

ASSUNTA, Bertuccio's sister-in-law.

BAPTISTIN, Monte Cristo's valet.

ALI, a Nubian mute, slave to Monte Cristo.

ABBÉ ADELMONTE, a Sicilian.

GERMAIN, Albert de Morcerf's valet.

ÉTIENNE, valet to Danglars.

BARROIS, Noirtier's servant.

FANNY, Mademoiselle de Villefort's maid.

PÈRE PAMPHILE, of La Réserve Inn.

CAPTAIN LECLERC, }
PENELON, a sailor, } in the service of M. Morell.
CAPTAIN GAUMARD, }

JOANNES, a jeweller.